EVERY MAN

for

HIMSELF

TEN SHORT STORIES ABOUT BEING A GUY

EVERY MAN
for HIMSELF
TEN SHORT STORIES ABOUT BEING A GUY

edited by Nancy E. Mercado

Paul Acampora
Edward Averett
Ron Koertge
David Levithan
David Lubar
Walter Dean Myers
René Saldaña, Jr.
Craig Thompson
Terry Trueman
Mo Willems

DIAL BOOKS

DIAL BOOKS
A member of Penguin Group (USA) Inc.
Published by The Penguin Group
Penguin Group (USA) Inc., 375 Hudson Street, New York, NY 10014, U.S.A.
Penguin Group (Canada), 10 Alcorn Avenue, Toronto, Ontario, Canada M4V 3B2
(a division of Pearson Penguin Canada Inc.)
Penguin Books Ltd, 80 Strand, London WC2R 0RL, England
Penguin Ireland, 25 St. Stephen's Green, Dublin 2, Ireland
(a division of Penguin Books Ltd)
Penguin Group (Australia), 250 Camberwell Road, Camberwell, Victoria 3124, Australia
(a division or Pearson Australia Group Pty Ltd)
Penguin Books India Pvt Ltd, 11 Community Centre, Panchsheel Park,
New Delhi - 110 017, India
Penguin Group (NZ), Cnr Airborne and Rosedale Roads, Albany, Auckland 1310,
New Zealand (a division of Pearson New Zealand Ltd)
Penguin Books (South Africa) (Pty) Ltd, 24 Sturdee Avenue, Rosebank,
Johannesburg 2196, South Africa
Penguin Books Ltd, Registered Offices: 80 Strand, London WC2R 0RL, England

Book design by Jasmin Rubero
Text set in Berkley
Printed in the U.S.A.

10 9 8 7 6 5 4 3 2

Library of Congress Cataloging-in-Publication Data
Every man for himself : ten short stories about being a guy /
edited by Nancy E. Mercado.
p.   cm.
Summary: An anthology of ten original short stories about
such things as family problems, sexuality, and courage, written by
well-known authors of children's books.
ISBN 0-8037-2896-4
1. Teenage boys—Juvenile fiction. 2. Children's stories, American.
[1. Boys—Fiction. 2. Teenagers—Fiction. 3. Interpersonal relations—Fiction.
4. Short stories.] I. Mercado, Nancy E., date.

PZ5.E927 2005

[Fic]—dc22 • 2004024069

TABLE OF CONTENTS

Introduction

I don't pretend to know or understand what guys are like in the slightest.

But I do trust other guys to know.

That's why I asked ten male authors whom I admire to contribute an original, fictional story that deals with what it's like to be a guy.

First, let me tell you what these stories are not. They are not stories about your voice changing, learning how to shave, or any other "coming-of-age" clichés like that.

These are real and honest stories about guys who are figuring stuff out and coming up with ways to deal with what life has thrown at them. Some of the stories are funny and some are kind of sad (don't say I didn't warn you!).

We've titled this collection *Every Man for Himself* because the truth is that there are always going to be times when you're on your own, when no one's around to help, and when it's up to you to decide what comes next.

Everyone knows that it's hard to come up with the best solution. Good news is, all of these authors have been there . . . and they're still around to tell about it.

Thanks for reading.

Nancy

THE PROM PRIZE

BY WALTER DEAN MYERS

You ever sit down, slip your body into relax mode, and just let your brain slide into deep chill? Like nothing is going on between your ears except maybe the background noise of your friends trying out some light rap about nothing in particular? Conversations go, like, "Yo, what's up?" and "Man, I hope Miss Evans don't check the English papers before she gives out the grades."

None of that meant anything, because everybody already knew what was up, which was nothing. And it was the end of the year, so everybody knew Miss Evans was going to check our papers before we got our grades. But that's what my homies were saying because they didn't have anything else to talk about. Then Tony

Sutherland, my main man, opened his mouth and turned the whole game around.

"Yo, Fly, you going to the junior prom?"

"Yeah, I guess." That was my cool reply.

"Who you going with?"

"I don't know, maybe I'll run a lottery," I said. "See who gets lucky."

That cracked Tony up. He started talking it around the school that I was going to run a lottery to see who got to go to the junior prom with me. Now, I'm not saying I'm all that special, but I ain't no sorry dude, either. Except sometimes I don't think things through too tough, especially when I don't see any danger. And I didn't see the danger coming at me, even when Tony got Amy Griffin to put an ad in the school paper.

WIN FLY WILLIAMS
FOR THE JUNIOR PROM

Eric "Fly" Williams, star forward for the Crusaders, is putting himself up for grabs in a lottery. The winning girl (or boy!) gets to go to the junior prom with the future NBA player. Put your name in the box at the newspaper office on the third floor. The drawing will be held next Thursday.

I liked that bit about the future NBA player because I think that's exactly where I'm headed. They call me Fly because that's exactly what I do when I'm on the court. So

I figured that a lot of the ladies would be slipping their names into the box. Also, since I didn't have a particular lady that I hung with, I thought it would be cool to see who showed up. It'd be like seeing what colleges offered me athletic scholarships.

So the whole thing was a big ha-ha, and they had the drawing, and guess who won. No lie, it was Bibi Overmeyer. Now, Bibi was all right, mind you. She was real tall for a girl, but she was kind of cute and had a nice smile. She was also smart enough to be offered a scholarship, as a junior, to Brown University. She was also white.

Now, not being of the white persuasion myself, I was still tolerant of all people, regardless of race, creed, or color. Check out my main dog, Tony. He plays forward on the school team, and he is also white. We hang together and we don't have any problems. So, when Bibi won the drawing, I was cool with it. But then Bibi put some crap in the game.

"So, look, I want to go to the prom with you," she said. "And I'll even go out with you afterward. But I don't do anything, if you know what I mean."

Well, yeah, I kind of knew what she meant, but I hadn't been thinking about, you know, doing anything. And that's where it would probably have stayed if I hadn't told Tony.

"Yo, man, why she have to say that?" Tony asked. "Just because you're a brother she has to assume you're going to hit on her?"

I didn't know why she said that, or why Tony was talking it up around the lunchroom. Tony has two things, a good inside game, and a big mouth. Soon, everybody was talking about how Bibi had told me she wasn't going to do anything.

"She's making stereotypical remarks about the black man in America." Gloria Jones had her hands on her hips and was doing the whole neck wiggling bit. "You have to tell her that if she can't accept you without a racist outlook, you're not going to the prom with her white butt!"

Now, everybody knew that Gloria was a militant. She even had the Koreans down at the mall paint her nails red, black, and green, the African liberation colors.

So the next time I saw Bibi in the hallway, I said that I kind of resented the idea that she had to warn me about her not doing anything. Bibi had heard all the talk too, and she was mad and told me that she was not a racist and if she was, she wouldn't have put her name in the box in the first place. That made sense to me and I was hoping it was going to end there. Bibi said that she was taking back what she had said before.

"Whatever happens," she said, "happens."

When Tony started rapping to me about how I should get on Bibi's case, I told him that I had already talked to Bibi and she had taken back what she had said and that she had added the bit about whatever happens, happens.

"She said that?" Tony asked.

"I just told you she did."

"So what you going to do?"

I didn't know what I was going to do, except to go to

the prom with Bibi, get through the night, and slide on into the summer. Then my pops got into the act.

"You need how much?" he asked.

"I think fifty dollars will do it," I said. "The junior prom is next week and I'm taking this girl, so I want to have some money in case we stop somewhere afterward."

"Who are you taking?" This from Mom.

"Bibi Overmeyer," I said, saying her name kind of quick. "You don't know her."

"Carole Overmeyer's daughter?" Mom asked, looking up from her magazine. "You know they all speak perfect German? It's nice for a family to stay in touch with their roots."

"German? If you're taking some white girl to the prom, you can't show up at her door without a ride," Pop said. "You need to rent a limousine."

"Then I guess I can't go," I said.

"I'll spring for it," Pop said. "Everybody is going to be looking at the Negro-White thing, so you have to be correct."

Just like that I got to be a Negro. The last time I saw the word was when we were studying the Civil Rights Movement in social studies. Now I was one and had to have Bibi in a limousine. It had been bad enough to have to go through all the stuff about what she was or was not going to do, now I had to represent the race as well. This was weak because I wasn't even sweating Bibi. She had won me in a drawing. This is what I tried to explain to Richie Scott.

Richie is a senior and our team's center. He thinks he's God's gift to the ladies and a basketball star. He's neither. The dude's too fat to run, and the only thing that keeps other centers from getting too close to him is his bad breath. But none of that stops him from telling everybody what they should be doing with their game or with their love life.

"If you springing for a limo, you got to throw some kisses on the chick and be ready in case anything sexual goes down," he said, his heavy arm around my shoulders and his bad breath slipping in my ear and probably messing up my brain. "You need to get to the drugstore and get some protection. You can't be having no babies holding back your NBA career."

"I'll go with you to the supermarket," Tony said, looking up from copying my homework. "We'll get some of those condoms that come in different colors."

"When am I going to have a chance to use them?" I asked. My palms were getting a bit sweaty. "How much can you make out in the backseat of the limo?"

"Suppose you take her home and she asks you in?" Tony said. "Her parents are asleep and you both tiptoe to her bedroom?"

"Yeah, yeah," Richie said, scratching his chin, "and she give you that look like the girl on television selling those indoor pools, man."

"Oh," I said. What I wanted to say was that Bibi already said she wasn't going to do anything, so there wasn't any need for me to buy any protection. Plus, I didn't know if I wanted to do anything. You had to be careful hitting on chicks in our school. One time Richie lucked a date with this cheerleader. They had gone to the movie and she got all into the flick and he tried to put his hand on her knee on the sly. Only he was pretending that he didn't realize where his hand was going and he put it on the girl's knee to his left instead of on the cheerleader's knee. The girl screamed on him right in the movie and then came to school the next day, told the whole story, and added that Richie had tried to kiss her in the elevator and his breath made her sick. That last part was probably true.

Bibi's parents were from Germany and I knew she had traveled a lot. I didn't know if she had much experience, but I didn't want to do anything stupid and then have her running her mouth about me. I mean, I wasn't afraid to make a mistake or anything, but there was already a lot going on, what with everybody knowing about us going out, plus the limousine.

So anyway, me and Tony go to the supermarket, hit the pharmacy aisles, and stop in front of the condoms. They have six different kinds and Tony's trying to pick out the right ones for me.

"What size you want?" he asks.

"I don't know," I said. "They got medium?"

"No, I mean you want a three-pack or like, a dozen?"

The three-pack looked safer, so I bought one and Tony bought one. They did have sizes, which were regular, large, and extra large. I wanted the large, because that was the middle size, but Tony said to get the extra large.

"You got to show her you're the man," he said. "When she sees the extra large, that's going to play with her mind."

So, I had everything covered. It was like the big game, maybe the championship of the city, maybe even of the world. The date with Bibi was set. I was going to have the limo. I had the condoms and I knew it couldn't last more than a few hours. I figured I pick her up at 7:00, get to the dance by 7:30, get our boogie on until 10:45, then get her back into the limo. We get to her house at 11:30 and she says I can't come in. Or maybe I can come in, but I make too much noise and her parents wake up. In fact, if they're decent parents, they won't even be asleep. I definitely was going to kiss Bibi, but I didn't want to sneak and do anything. Then I'd go home and everything would be cool.

Along comes Monday morning and Tony drops his condoms in the cafeteria. Right in the middle of the table where he's sitting with Bobby Scott, Joel from the band, Sarah Upton, and big mouth Mary Acosta. From fifteen feet away you could hear Bobby asking what Tony's doing with the condoms. Everybody turned to look and Bobby's holding them up in the air and Tony's talking and pointing over toward where I was sitting putting ketchup on my french fries one by one like I always do. I was trying to figure out what was going on and then I saw Mary get this funny expression on her face and then she was getting up and going over to where Bibi Overmeyer was sitting.

As I said, Bibi is tall, at least six feet, and it doesn't take her more than about six long steps to get over to where I was sitting. And I didn't have to be 007 to figure out what was on her mind.

"Excuse me, Mr. Williams," she said. "I understand you only bought three condoms for prom night. Are you sure that's going to be enough?"

"Yo, Bibi, I don't know what you're talking about," I said. "I saw Mary Acosta chewing on your ear, but she ain't the six o'clock news as far as I'm concerned. If I need to say something to you, I'll just come say it."

"You've got a lot of high hopes for this date, haven't you?" Bibi asked.

"I just hope we can both have a good time," I said.

"You mess with me and you're going to get more than you bargained for." Bibi's finger was at the tip of my nose. "And I'm still not backing out so you can call me a racist!"

I had already gotten more than I'd bargained for. So when Richie came up and started talking about how Bibi, being white and all, was afraid of the black man, I really wasn't ready to hear it.

"Throughout history, white people have been secretly afraid of us!" he said.

This whole thing had started out to be a cool way of getting a prom date, but it had escalated into about nine other things. I was renting a limo because my pops had me representing the race, I was buying extra-large condoms to show I was the man, and now I had the whole junior class waiting to see what was going to happen. What I needed was a time-out and a new game plan.

9

"You've got to be strong. You're representing all of us. The men against the women!" This from Richie.

"Make sure she sees the box with the size on it!" This from Tony.

"Make sure you let the limo driver open the door for the young lady!" This from Pop.

"Do you think she wants to go to the dance with you because her parents are going to be out of town on junior prom night?" This from Mary Acosta, Miss Mala Prensa, who swore she had gotten the scoop straight from one of the women who work in the lunchroom.

The days flew by almost as fast as the rumors about what was going to happen between me and Bibi on prom night. I wasn't too uptight about the night itself. It was the instant replay when I got to school that worried me. Since I was representing almost everybody in the free world, I knew there were going to be a bunch of questions.

Night of the junior prom. I was nervous, but I was laughing it off. I got dressed and checked myself out in the mirror. Okay, the kid was looking good. Teeth brushed, lots of deodorant, just the right touch of Pop's aftershave. Mom was shedding a Mom tear. Pop was giving me the elbow and saying not to do anything that he wouldn't do, whatever that meant. The phone rang at 6:20 and I figured it was Bibi saying she didn't want to go to the prom with me. I fixed my mind to handle it, but it was only the limo driver saying he was outside waiting for me.

No big deal, I told myself. I took the corsage out of the

vegetable drawer and went out to the limo. The driver nodded when he saw me and opened the door. I had my game face on and my game plan in mind. I was going to play it super cool. Pick Bibi up and talk about the situation in the Middle East while we're in the limo. I'd get the tall mama to the dance, swing her around the floor a couple of times, then when things wound down, I'd pick up Tony and a couple of other kids, whisk them out for a late spin in the limo, then drop off everybody except Bibi. Take Bibi home, throw a polite kiss on her, and then—the debonair move—ask her politely if she wanted to "do anything else." Just like that.

"Do you want to do anything else?"

"No, I don't!"

"Then bonsoir, ma cherie!"

Then I give my head a little shake, kiss Bibi's hand, and split like I was too sophisticated to even worry about it. Which I was.

When I got to Bibi's house, her parents were just leaving. I met them on the driveway to her house. They had a small suitcase with them. Uh-oh. Mary Acosta was right. I took a deep breath as her dad looked me up and down carefully. He shook my hand and showed me a firm grip. Her mother gave me this half smile and bowed her head a little.

"Bibi's waiting for you," she said. "Have a nice time."

Then they left and I rang the doorbell. There was no answer at first and I'm thinking that Bibi was chickening out. Then the door opened and she was standing in the doorway looking like a goddess. Word! She was looking fine in this black gown that just barely kept her lungs in and clung to her body like it was happy to be doing it! My eyes liked to fell out and I was standing there grinning with my mouth open. I had to look stupid.

"Hi, Fly," she said.

"Uh, hi." My suave reply.

Bibi got her jacket and we got into the limo. I couldn't think of anything to say about the Middle East, and then I come up with a really good idea of talking about what a nice day it was and was just about ready to lay that on her when her knee touched mine and I lost my train of thought.

We got to the dance and everybody was scoping how fab Bibi looked. Everybody's checking us out. Dudes I didn't even know were winking at me and giving me the high sign. We're dancing some fast stuff and I'm all good because I got the moves to fit the groove, but Bibi's got some moves too. She's also hip to the beat, so we got a little show thing going on and she's smiling, so everything is all right. There's a little break while some teacher is making noise about drinking and driving and Bibi says she has to go to the ladies' room.

"Yo, man, after the intermission the band is going to play some slow stuff," Tony says. "You can tell what she's thinking by how she slow dances."

Meanwhile, I don't see Tony dancing with anybody and all Richie is doing is guarding the punch bowl. Now, I'm down with fast dancing, but I really don't know them slow numbers and I get a little nervous. I'm thinking about checking out Lost and Found to see if anybody had picked up my cool in the parking lot or wherever I left it.

So here we go. Slow dancing. Me and Bibi are in the middle of the floor and all my homies and a few gnomies are right around us scoping us out. I decided to just shut my mind, put my arms around the girl, forget about everybody watching, and get through it the best way I could. Why did she have to hum in my ear?

Bibi started humming in my ear and rubbing the back of my neck with one finger. She was definitely messing with my mind. Her touch was real light too—a shoulder brushed against mine, a little hip rub, our chests touched for a half second just as her lips touched my cheek, and she was steady humming. Thoughts were flying around my head like balls in a Ping-Pong tournament, and my heart was making some funny moves of its own. When the first slow dance ended and we sat down, my knees were ready to give out.

The next number was a reggae and Bibi danced with a teacher. Richie came over and told me he had thought about cutting in and had changed his mind.

"I saw the way you were working your show and I didn't want to ruin it for you, man," he said. "Yeah, nice looking out, bro."

Then the last dance came. I found out that most of my crowd was going over to the next town and Bibi said she had to get home because her parents were going to call at one. I hadn't even realized that it was nearly twelve.

We get into the limo and she snuggled up against me and started thanking me for a nice time, and I was thanking her for a nice time and we're thanking each other until we got to her house. It was about six miles from the limo to her front door, but somehow I made it.

"You wanna . . . ?"

"No," she said. Then she kissed me. Her face was already close to mine when she was standing, so I didn't expect the kiss when it came and I didn't know exactly what to do when it lasted a little longer than I thought it would. Well, maybe a lot longer. Just about the time I started thinking about where I might put my hands, it was over.

"Hey, you want to go out again?" I asked as she backed into the doorway.

She reached into her purse and pulled out her cell phone and held it up.

Yes, I definitely was going to call her.

Monday, after basketball practice.

"Yo, man, you got to tell us what happened!" Richie said. We were in the locker room. Tony was leaning against the lockers with a towel around his neck and four other guys from the team were there.

"Nothing happened," I said.

"Not according to Mary Acosta," Richie said. "She said she asked Bibi how it went and Bibi just closed her eyes and said you really know how to kiss. Why did she have to close her eyes, man? She must have been thinking about what you did. What was she thinking about?"

"I don't know." I shrugged.

Afterward, when we were walking home, Tony said I was right in not telling everybody what had happened.

"That shows you're not just a kid getting all excited about being with a woman and whatnot," he said. "I've always thought that black dudes were cool like that."

Yeah, I guess we are.

JUMP AWAY

BY RENÉ SALDAÑA, JR.

Fenny clung to the metal railing behind him. The cement ledge under him was hot on his bare feet. He looked down at the river and nodded. Easy enough, he thought. Not scary like in all those movies where the manly-man hero's scaling an impossible mountainside to escape an enemy, or walking across a rotting wooden bridge high-high, way above a rushing river, in search of the ever-illusive treasure, and someone else, the sidekick or the sarcastic native guide, says, "Whatever you do, don't look down," and always, always the "hero" (who it turns out is afraid of heights) does look down and freezes stiff or makes some kind of 'fraidy-cat remark that usually makes audiences laugh.

Fenny wasn't scared that way. He wasn't bothered by heights. That's not why he was clinging to the bridge railing. He just didn't want to go in before Mike said so. That'd mean certain trouble for him at school. Today was their turn, six or seven of them, all the oddballs on campus, challenged to jump from Jensen's Bridge to prove themselves to Mike and the rest of his numb-nut crew of strong-arms.

Fenny looked up—upriver, some hundred, hundred fifty yards—and saw two people . . . fishing? Yeah, fishing, he figured. Fenny couldn't see the rods themselves, much less the lines, but how the two sat and held out their arms, their reeling in and casting motions told him that's what they were about.

"Any of you want to chicken out?" asked Mike. He was also hanging on to the rail, several jumpers to Fenny's left. Mike swung out, holding on with one hand, and looked at the rest of them, a smile on his face, but a glare too. Mike had been in charge at school of recruiting the "next batch," what he called those who he felt needed to show they were real men, "not the skinny-punk-knuckleheads I think you really are." At school this last week, Mike and his boys had surrounded the would-be jumpers one at a time and told them, "Jump, or be jumped." Every one of the boys Mike confronted during the past week showed up today. "Any of you girls want to back out? It's okay if you do. Not all of us have to be man enough. How about you, Femmy? You look a bit shaky." He laughed.

Fenny said, "It's Fenny, and don't worry about me. I'm jumping. I'm just waiting for the word." He let go one hand to brush back his hair.

Mike humphed. "And the rest of you punks, what's it going to be? Any of you others wanna punk out?"

No one said anything.

Fenny wasn't afraid, but even so he really didn't want to jump. No, really he did, but on his own terms, not forced like what Mike was doing to them here. He wanted to go when he wanted. Better yet, he would've liked to've been fishing instead, like the two people upriver. He looked at them again, and he saw one of them standing up, looking in their direction, a girl with her hand cupped over her eyes. She was wearing a sleeveless shirt, her arms looked pinkish to Fenny. The day was good for fishing: warm enough, almost no current to speak of.

Fenny pulled a stick of gum from his shorts pocket. What am I doing here? he thought. What do I care what Mike thinks about me? Fenny remembered a story he'd read recently in class about a boy who's been challenged to dive fifty feet from a ledge into a pool of water at the base of a waterfall. The boy in the story doesn't dive, instead treks back down to the base where the others, a girl included, figure him for a wimp. Fenny thought, Easy for a kid to do in a story, who doesn't have to worry about a very real thug like Mike, whose very real fists mean very real bruises and black eyes and a bloody nose.

"Last chance," said Mike.

Fenny considered climbing back over the railing, walking down to the riverbank, up to the people fishing, and asking, "How're they biting?" Maybe sitting down beside one of them and saying, "What about you giving me a turn?" then casting his line and lazy-lazy reeling it back in, no matter nothing was biting, but the sun on his face and arms would be good. But then he'd remember Monday was just around the corner, and everyone would know at school he hadn't jumped, so he'd get beaten up, or worse, Mike or someone else would pull his pants down around his ankles and shove him down in the hall between periods and everyone would laugh, the girls would giggle at his skinny legs, point at his tight white underpants while he tried covering himself with one hand and with the other try to pull his pants up, not one sympathetic girl in the bunch, not one who would come up to him after to say, "Listen, Fenny, these guys are jerks blah blah blah." Nope, just laughing.

Forget the fishing, he thought. "So, what? Are we jumping or are you yapping?" Fenny said. He turned and looked at Mike. When Fenny saw Mike's ugly stare, he knew that even if he jumped today, he'd still be Femmy at school and Mike would still be the bozo who pushed him around. It's not like we'll be best of friends come Monday, he thought.

"Whoa," Mike said, "anxious, are we? Just hold your horses, Femmy. It'll happen soon enough. I just need to work some psychology-mumbo-jumbo on the rest of your buddies. One of them, at least one of them, will back down if we wait up here long enough. Right? Who's first to pansy out? It's not going to be Femmy by the sound of him. So who's it going to be? How about you, Ritchie? No? You? Or you?" Mike went down the line, calling each of the boys by name, waiting six or seven seconds, all the time staring at them. Not one of them backed down, though.

"Impressive. Okay, then, on the count of three. Ready? On my three. One," said Mike.

To heck with it, Fenny thought. I'm going in early, on my own. Mike or no Mike.

"Two," and right before he called *three,* Fenny said, "Three," and jumped, toes pointed right at the water. He took a breath and kept his eyes open. It looked to him like the fishing-girl was looking their way. Fenny stiffened and cut right into the water, no problem. He breathed hard out of his nose on impact. Then he was under, murky and green down there. He heard the others' muffled screams, then the gurgling of them breaking the water. Fenny went all the way down, down far enough to feel the slimy bottom of the river oozing between his toes, his eyes open the whole way, his eyes bulging from the pressure, his eyes stinging from keeping them open.

He pushed himself off the river bottom and shot up and out of the water. The others swam to the bank. Mike was already out and shaking himself off. Then a couple joined him, then the rest. All of them looking for a place to lie down. Fenny took his time, though, flipped over and swam on his back.

"Couldn't wait, could you?" Mike screamed.

Fenny swung his arm up over his body in a perfect arc

and sliced his hand into the water, then reached way, way down and felt the river with his knuckles under him. He'd almost reached the edge, and so he stood up, water up to his knees pushing against him. He saw the others, everyone except for Mike, lying down in the sun. Mike glared at him. "I said go on three. My three. Not two, not two and a half. And definitely not your three. That too difficult a plan for you?" See, things hadn't changed much. Mike was still a jerk.

"Easy enough plan. Your three, not mine. You were just taking your sweet time, though. Like you were having a hard time figuring what came after two."

Fenny saw the others tilt their heads up and in his direction. One or two of them leaned up on an elbow. Mike inched his way up to Fenny, the whole time his chest sticking out, his slicked-back hair shining in the sun. "What'd you say?" Now the two were up on each other, face-to-face. Breathing heavy. "I know you just didn't speak out of turn. And I know you didn't just say what I think I heard you say. Right?"

Fenny was quiet.

Then he said, "No, you heard me right."

The speed of what happened next caught Fenny off guard, but it didn't surprise him. Mike's fist caught him full on the left side of his face, right on the cheekbone, and Fenny was down on the ground.

"You know," said Mike, "you diving today, it doesn't change anything."

Of course it doesn't, thought Fenny. Why would it?

NO MORE BIRDS WILL DIE TODAY

BY PAUL ACAMPORA

"Charlie," Liam yells. "Charlie, the Grinch is on in seven minutes!"

Liam is my younger brother. He's parked in front of the TV, and I'm drying dishes in the kitchen with Chevy. Chevy's our dad.

"Okay," I holler.

"Here," Chevy says, handing me a plate.

Chevy's got on his rattiest jeans, his oil-soaked work boots, and a faded Jack Daniel's T-shirt. He insists on clean dishes, but he's not afraid to break a few if it helps him to make a point now and then. "Last one," he says.

"Yeah."

He gives me a look, probably trying to decide whether

or not I'm being disrespectful. The beers he had over supper put him in a good mood, though, so he lets it go.

I dry the dish and return it to the cupboard. I'm tall and lanky like Chevy, so I can see everything on our shelves. We've got three dinner plates, three dessert plates, three bowls, and three mugs. We're the Three god-damn Bears.

"Four minutes!"

"Okay, Liam." I start pulling down bowls and popcorn and chips. Liam's been waiting all week to see the Grinch.

"I can't believe they still show the dumb thing," Chevy says.

"It's a classic," I tell him.

"It's stupid."

"It's not stupid," Liam yells from the other room.

"Jesus Christ," Chevy mutters. "The boy can hear a mouse fart in a bowling alley."

Liam just turned seven. I'll be fifteen in June, but I tell you, I can't keep up with that kid. He's wound up so tight, it wears you out just to look at him. He's got these intense blue eyes, and no matter what he's wearing, it's wrinkled and flapping around behind him like some kind of crazy kite. His hair is dirty blond, and it sticks straight up as if electricity had just shot out of his head a minute ago. He doesn't look anything like Chevy or me, so he's figured that he must take after our mother, who, as far as Liam knows, died when he was a baby. A sudden tragic heart attack, we tell him. God took her away. The truth is, it was a man named Harold who took her away. He was

23

an orderly at the nursing home where she used to work. She left with him when I was nine.

"What do you think," Chevy asked me when it happened. We were sitting in a McDonald's and my brother, just a baby then, was asleep against Chevy's sleeve. "If you were Liam, would you rather have a dead mother or a mother who took off?"

I thought about it hard. I picked the last greasy fry out of the box before I said, "Dead mother."

"Yeah," said Chevy, rubbing Liam a little. "Getting dumped this early could really screw a kid up." He looked down at the baby. "Dead mother it is."

We should have told Liam the real story because, as it works out, he is loony tunes anyway.

Take his ideas about firemen. When Liam was five, I gave him a book about fire trucks. What kid doesn't like fire trucks? Liam let me read the book to him before bed, and at the end he says, "I don't know what I'll be when I grow up, but I know I'll never be a fireman."

I know that I should let it go, but I just can't help myself. "Liam," I say. "Why don't you want to be a fireman?"

He has to take a big breath before he can answer. "Charlie," he says. "When I jumped down from the fire engine, I would look at some family's house burning, and you know, that would be so very sad."

This is exactly what he says to me. "That would be so very sad."

"I wouldn't be able to get the hose or the ladders or

anything," he continues. "I think I would just stand there and cry."

"Liam," I say, "firemen are heroes. They save people. It's good when the firemen come."

One big tear is running down Liam's face. "No, Charlie. No. By then it's too late." He takes another breath, trying to calm down.

"It's okay," he says. He's mostly talking to himself now. "It's okay. If we have a fire, I can just run and grab my things and get them out of the house."

I have to tell you that our father falls asleep on the couch, cigarette in hand, just about every night. We have this old green sofa in the living room. The cushions look like the surface of the moon, pockmarked black from Lucky Strikes. I can't let Liam go to bed thinking it's okay to pack a suitcase while the house burns down around him, because I know that's just what he'd do.

"Liam, what are you supposed to do if there's a fire?"

Liam looks away from me. I'm sure he's making a mental checklist of every item in the house that needs to be rescued.

"Liam," I say again. "What are you supposed to do if there's a fire?" He knows the answer. He's the one that made us practice the damn evacuation plan for Fire Safety Week last year. I grab his shoulders and give him a shake. "Liam, answer me!"

I feel him sag a little in my hands, and now he's really crying. "I know, I know," he says. "Go outside. Go to the end of the driveway. Meet at the mailbox." He stops and begins to wail. "And then we all stand together and watch the house burn down." He buries his face into my shoulder and sobs.

"Liam. Liam, it's okay. We're not going to have a fire." I say this with complete confidence while I make a mental note to check on Chevy and the couch and every ashtray in the house before I go to bed for the rest of my life. "Liam," I say, "as long as we have each other, we'll be fine. There's nothing in this house that we can't buy new."

Liam wipes his nose on his pajama sleeve. "Charlie," he says. "I don't want anything new. When the firemen leave, I want to just come back in and scrape the black stuff off my old toys. Okay?"

What the hell am I supposed to say to that?

"Sure," I say. "Yes, Liam. That would be fine. Okay. Go to sleep now. Sweet dreams. Good night."

The Grinch is about to begin. Chevy's settling into his second six-pack and that old Grinchy voice starts. "Every Who down in Whoville liked Christmas a lot . . . " In no time, Liam is deep into it. To tell you the truth, so am I.

Chevy doesn't say much. This could be good, but with Chevy, you never know. Chevy isn't too much like other dads we know. First off, he makes us call him Chevy. Everyone calls him Chevy. This bothers Liam to no end because most of the time, Chevy drives a big red Mack truck. He parks the rig on the side of the house.

Our house was built by Chevy's grandfather about a hundred years ago. You've probably seen it, the white, clapboard Colonial with a massive sycamore out front. It's in all the Connecticut tourist guides and calendars. Chevy's always talking about suing somebody because we've never given anyone permission to take photos of the place.

Chevy can be a lot of fun. He also has a mean streak in him that's a mile wide. Like last April, he bought BB guns for the three of us.

We were at school, and he was in between long hauls. He must have spent the whole day setting up tin cans and targets in the backyard. Liam and I ride the school bus, and when we got to the back porch that afternoon, there was Chevy, ready to show us the whole setup, guns and all.

Chevy tells us, "These are Crossman bolt-action pump rifles." They've got dark steel barrels and solid wood stocks. Chevy shows us how to load the little copper pellets and line up the sites. Ten or twelve strokes on the pump, and they're ready to go. I tell you, we just about lose our minds.

The amazing thing is that right away, Liam is a natural sharpshooter. The first time he looks down the barrel of his gun, he has the whole thing figured out. He hits every tin can, every bull's-eye, every target we set up. I tape a quarter to the side of a chestnut tree about thirty yards off the porch. Liam puts a dimple right on George Washington's nose.

Somehow, this ticks Chevy off. He gets this look on his face, the look of a trucker that maybe just got cut off by a Volkswagen, and he starts taking pot shots at the finches and sparrows that hang around our yard. The birds gather around these junky feeders that Liam slaps together in our basement. There's probably twenty plastic and wood seed baskets dangling all over the place, so you can always find a few scrappy birds nearby.

I've got to say that Chevy's a pretty good shot himself. Before you know it, there's half a dozen dead and bleeding birds lying in the grass. Liam is screaming bloody murder yelling, "Stop! Stop!" He's running around the backyard trying to pick up the wounded birds. The ones that aren't unconscious are half crazed by now, and they're just pecking holes in Liam's bare hands. I hear Chevy's gun making that *pofft, pofft, pofft, pofft* and three more birds—two blue jays and a blackbird—fall right out of the sky.

Meanwhile, I've discovered that I'm one of these people that couldn't hit the side of a barn even if I had a cannon. That's okay. Chevy's only two feet away. I don't even hesitate. I put three quick shots into his ass, and I'm thinking, Did I really just shoot my father?

"Son of a bitch!" Chevy roars.

He drops his gun, grabs his seat, and starts hopping around. Liam is running back toward the porch. Chevy is cursing up a storm, and I'm pretty sure that he's going to rip the heart right out of my chest.

He finally stops jumping and swearing, but he doesn't go for me. He just sort of takes stock of the situation. Liam is covered with blood. Flesh and feathers litter the backyard. I've got the Crossman pointed at Chevy's eyeball.

"Whoa," Chevy says, and raises his hands like this is a stickup.

"That's enough," I yell at him. "No more. No more birds will die today."

Chevy backs toward the screen door and limps into the house. "You got me," he hollers from the bathroom. "You got me good, Charlie. Really good. You're a winner. You win."

After he cleans and bandages his backside, Chevy retreats into the kitchen. He makes supper. He makes ravioli, my favorite. "It's a feast," he says, looking at me, "a feast for you, Charlie, our top marksman, our champion. How does it feel to be a big man, Charlie?"

I don't answer. I eat the ravioli. I eat every one, and every one tastes like bones and beaks and dirt, and we never talk about that day again.

The Grinch has the sleigh teetering at the edge of the mountain, Mount Crumpet. He's packed up all the toys and food and decorations, and he's going to dump it.

Liam is on the edge of his seat. Actually, so am I, even though I know that in just a minute, Christmas is going to get into that Grinch's heart and turn him into some kind of holy super Santa hero. I know it, but when a story is really good, I sort of lose my mind. I can hear it a hundred times, and I'll still worry, How's it going to turn out?

So there we are, having one of our rare family moments. Me and Liam are stuffed with popcorn. Chevy's flipping bottle caps toward the kitchen door, and the Grinch is about to get that I-think-I-found-Jesus look and save the day. That's when Chevy clears his throat. He sits himself up and he informs us, "Boys, here comes the bullshit part."

All of a sudden I'm embarrassed, because, you know what—Chevy is kind of right. And I'm angry. I'm angry at everybody, even Doctor Seuss. I mean, crumpet dump-it, floozit snooze-it. What the hell is he even talking about?

When I get this way, I should just run and run until I find a pool and jump into it or a blanket and pull it over my head. What I should not do is speak, but I look right at Chevy and I say, "Remember the one about Rudolph the red-nosed reindeer?" That takes him by surprise, but I go on. "Santa almost cancels Christmas because of bad weather. They live at the goddamn North Pole. Shouldn't they be used to bad weather?"

Chevy barks out a quick laugh before he gets his face under control. "Hey, watch your mouth," he says. Then he smiles. "You want a beer?"

The Grinch is cutting up the roast beast. Chevy is laughing under his breath. Liam has left the room, and I didn't even notice him go. I swear, I am such an asshole.

I wonder if Liam is still angry. We haven't spoken in two days, and now I've followed him outside. He's standing on top of a fallen maple in the woods behind our house. There's a pond farther back and the foundation to a barn that burned down ages ago.

Liam doesn't see me, and he calls to the trees, *"Helloooo!"* His voice rolls through the branches until the moss and leaves swallow it up. He yells again, *"Hellooo!"*

Liam skips through a clearing. He's poking under logs, running along the top of the old stone wall that cuts through our property. There's a stick in his hand, and he's waving it in the air.

When I was little, I'd walk back here with Mom. She'd laugh at me with a dry branch in my hand trying to tell the leaves and the squirrels how to behave. "There's nothing better than being in the woods with a good stick," she'd say. I think she was right.

Mom would tell me stories, not stupid stories but real stories. She told me things that were true, like all these woods used to be farmland. Some crazy farmer and his sons spent years cutting trees and clearing stones to make fields. They piled up rocks in long, straight heaps to mark the edges of their land.

"No matter how many rocks you pull out of this dirt," Mom told me once, "the earth will keep spitting up more." It has something to do with frost and glaciers and geology.

That old farmer didn't know. He probably believed that he and his boys could clear every last stone. I think about me and Liam and Chevy. What if we were farmers? In the spring, when Chevy's plow smacked another big black rock, I wonder how much of a beating I'd get.

To top it off, the field that was here is forest again. Probably a hundred winters have passed since anybody put a seed in this ground. If you stick a shovel into the earth ten times in these woods, you're going hit a stone with every stroke.

I can't see Liam anymore. He probably caught sight of me standing around daydreaming. The bottom edge of the sun is just touching the western ridgeline. Sunbeams wash through the trees like searchlights. It's cold, but a few leftover leaves still cling to mostly bare branches. They shine in gaudy reds and yellows and orange. A twig snaps behind me, but I pretend that I don't hear it.

"Charlie," Liam calls from somewhere in the trees. "I see you. What do you want?"

I don't answer. I imagine my brother perched on a branch somewhere behind me. I don't turn around. If I do, he'll fly away. "I'm sorry," I finally yell into the woods. "I'm really sorry."

Suddenly, he's racing through the trees. I hear *shish-shish-shish,* his feet flying through the leaves. The sound is like a thousand wings, angels and vultures sweeping down on me from out of the winter sky.

I turn. Liam is almost on top of me. He's got that stick out in front like a soldier with a bayonet. "Hey!" I yell, stumbling backward. "Stop!"

I've fallen on the ground, and Liam is above me. He reaches out with the stick and brushes it against my cheek, almost into my eye. It's sharp, but it tickles a little, and I can smell dirt and moss on the bark.

"Why are you following me?" Liam asks, poking me a little with the stick.

"I don't know," I yell, and I'm thinking, This is not my

job. This is not going well. My mother should be here. She should be telling Liam all the stories, the stories about the farmer, the stones, our home, our family, or at least Chevy could be telling both of us one true thing once in a while.

"Well?" Liam asks, poking me again. His pants have ridden up his skinny ankles. His Windbreaker is unzipped and bunched up behind him.

"Liam," I ask. "Do you remember Mom?"

He glares at me, confused. "No," he says. "God took Mom. God took her. I was little."

I shake my head. I'm tired. I'm tired of everything, and I look at Liam. He's all puffed full of anger and lies like a hot-air balloon about to pull away from the landscape. For one scary second I want to burst that balloon. Keep him on the ground. Scream in his face, God did not take Mom. She just flew. She just flew away.

But as fast as the urge to hurt him appears, I shove it down. I swallow it, and it burns like kerosene in my stomach and in my throat. I want to spit it out, but I hold it inside me. I feel it there, and I think, This is what dragons must taste before they incinerate princes and castles.

I stare hard at my brother until finally I say, "You know, Mom used to tell me stories. She told me stories about these woods."

"How would I know?" Liam says.

He's right. How would he know? He is still angry, but I see the point of the stick lower a little. His face is a fading storm, not calm yet, but maybe not so dangerous as it was a moment ago.

I close my eyes. I do not open them again until I speak. "If you want," I say. "Maybe I can tell you."

"Tell me what?" Liam asks.

I stare at his face. I do not know what I am going to say. When the words come out of my mouth, it will be like watching a long train emerge from a dark tunnel. I don't know which car will come next. I hear myself speak, and the words move me forward as if I know where it is that I am going.

"A story," I say. "Maybe I can tell you a story."

SHOCKERS

BY DAVID LUBAR

Delia shrieked like she was being gutted with a dull butter knife. Oh boy. I knew that scream. I knew it well. It was the one that announced earthshaking news.

We were up in her room. Her folks were pretty cool about that, as long as we kept the door cracked an inch or two, though her mom generally popped her head in at random intervals to ask if we wanted a cup of hot chocolate or to inform us about the topic for the evening's *Nightline*.

Her dad glanced in our direction if he happened to be walking down the hall, though he didn't talk much. Our longest conversation took place the first time we met. I'll give him this—he didn't blink. I think my hair was pink that week. Can't remember for sure. I had the earrings, the nose ring, and the one in my lip, but I hadn't gotten my eyebrow pierced yet. Delia's dad lifted his right hand, pointed at my cheek, and said, "Steve, I think you missed a spot." Very funny.

Back to the scream. It was Friday night, around eleven. I was hanging out, reading *Neuromancer* for the ninth or tenth time. The book was one of the summer reading assignments for senior English, which I took as a good sign. Delia was downloading the latest top-forty samples, exchanging instant messages with her friends, and surfing for fashion news to make sure the pants she'd bought two days ago were still in style.

After the scream, Delia leaped from her chair and clapped her hands together like someone killing a bee. As much as I disliked the scream, I loved the way everything moved when she jumped. She was in great shape. She didn't just turn heads. She snapped them. Last week, I swear I saw a guy in the mall do a one-eighty from the neck up. I could almost hear vertebrae separating. Of course, the fact that her skirt could be mistaken for a belt added to the impact.

"Steve, you'll never guess," she said.

"Martians invaded the mall?" I asked, placing my book facedown to save my place.

"No. Guess who's playing at the Dome."

I replayed her scream through my mind and knew the answer. And, with the answer, all the consequences. My fate was sealed. Life would suck for two hours at some point in the future. Why couldn't love be deaf? Ungritting my teeth, I spoke their name. "Oh! Golly."

"Yeah. Oh! Golly," she said. "They're playing at the Dome next month. Tickets go on sale Monday."

"Oh great," I said. Softly. As the posters that were plastered across her walls testified, Delia was their number one fan. I didn't share her enthusiasm. Oh! Golly was one of those bands that, like Frankenstein's monster, have been sewn together by an evil genius. They weren't created in a gas-fumed garage by a group of musicians who'd known each other since birth. They sprang from the depths of a record company's marketing department. Their music was upbeat. Their lives were wholesome. Between the five members of the group, they had enough shiny white teeth to tile a spacious bathroom. The title of their latest album was *Puppy Chuckles*. Kill me now.

Delia dashed across the room and hugged me. "I'm so excited. We are going to have the best time." She kept her grip while jumping up and down. Had I been lighter, I would have left the ground. As it was, I could feel part of my body rising. Okay, kill me later. I reached up to return the embrace.

"You kids want ice cream?" Delia's mom inserted the front portion of her head into the room. "I've got mocha almond fudge and peanut butter swirl."

"No thanks, Mrs. Kensington," I said as I stepped away from Delia and tried to wipe all signs of passion off my face.

"Well, let us know if you change your mind." She withdrew and moved silently away along the thick carpet in the hall.

Delia ran back to her computer. I ran various escape options through my mind. Maybe she wouldn't be able to get tickets. Maybe the whole band would come down with food poisoning. Maybe I'd break both legs in a snowboarding accident. Okay, not likely in the middle of June, but a guy could hope.

As much as I loved to visit my fantasy world where I could imagine entire bands suddenly struck down with a hideously painful gum disease, I realized I was out of luck. Delia always got what she wanted, whether it was a new outfit, concert tickets, or any guy on the planet. Her dad made good money doing some sort of thing with municipal bonds. Her mom came from a family that once owned a chain of movie theaters. Delia was an only child. The Kensingtons had nobody else to spoil.

I'm not poor, but my life wasn't anything like Delia's. We moved in different circles. Possibly even in different universes. But we're both good artists. Very good, actually. So we couldn't help running into each other all the time in the art room. I could tell Delia didn't want to admit that some freaky guy with spiked hair and a face full of hardware could draw like a Renaissance master. And I wasn't willing to accept that some egocentric chick with perfect makeup and coordinated outfits could paint circles around the French Impressionists. But there it was. And there we were.

I stayed after school a lot to work on stuff. One day, when Delia and I were leaving at the same time, we started talking. The next day, we talked and grabbed a burger. I noticed that she didn't stare at me like I was some sort of freak. And I tried my hardest not to stare at her like she was some sort of cover girl. I might have failed slightly in my efforts, but it didn't seem to bother her. She knew she was hot.

There was a Gustave Klimt exhibit opening at the art museum that weekend. None of my friends wanted to go. None of her friends wanted to go. So she and I went. I guess that was our first date. I figured we'd meet at the museum, but she asked me to pick her up at her place. Said her parents insisted on it. So that's when I first met her folks. It was actually sort of nice. The last couple girls I'd gone out with had tried to hide me from their parents. We'd had a good time at the museum.

Now here I was, more than a month later, still with her. I got ready to head home at 11:45. I have this stupid junior license, so I can't be on the road after midnight. "Hey, I'm glad you're going to get to see them," I told Delia. That was true. I understood the passion, even if I loathed the target.

"Thanks." She stood and put a hand on my shoulder. "I'm glad we're going too."

I leaned forward to give her a kiss.

Tap.

Bam!

Tap. Tap.

BamBamBam!

I peered around the door. The culprit was Mrs. Kensington in the hallway with a hammer.

"Family photos," she said as she lifted a huge frame onto the hanger she'd just nailed to the wall. "Been meaning to put this up for weeks. Come see."

I came and saw. The newly hung object was one of those photo displays with a bunch of holes cut in a mat board. Lots of snapshots of Delia at various ages in various outfits. All adorable. Faded shots of grandparents. Assorted adults in pairs and groups. One picture caught my eye. Mr. Kensington and Delia with fishing rods, standing by a lake. She's five or six, and grinning. He's holding a fish.

I noticed him coming down the hall—probably to make sure the wall was still standing. "Smallmouth?" I asked, pointing at the picture.

He nodded. "Seventeen inches. I hooked it, but Delia landed it. You fish?"

"I used to. With my dad. It's been a while." Wow. A conversation.

"Delia hasn't fished in a while, either," he said.

She made a sound that indicated she had no immediate plans to ruin her streak.

"Well, I'd better get going." I didn't want to have him start asking about my dad. He'd died way back. I could deal with that. But the sad eyes and all that crap when people found out—I didn't need that.

Delia walked me to the door. Behind us, I heard her mother say, "He's such a nice boy." She said that a lot, usually right after pulling her eyes away from the Persistence-of-Memory tattoo that covered my right arm.

40

But she was getting better. The first time she saw me, her face assumed the expression of someone who just realized she's swallowed a live millipede.

I managed to get that kiss on the porch, then drove home, with the new Smothered Guppies CD blasting loud enough to scrape any thoughts of Oh! Golly from my mind.

Hope number one on my list of escape routes was dashed on Monday. Delia hit the phone the instant tickets went on sale and scored seats so close, we'd be able to count tonsils. Hot diggity. She bought the limit.

"Six tickets?" I asked when she told me the news.

"Sure. We're all going," she said. "Suzie and Candace love Oh! Golly. Everything's set."

And it was. No freak summer blizzards struck. No crazed fans kidnapped the group. I didn't break a single limb. The time had come. We were going to the concert of her dreams. My mom dropped me off at Delia's house. I'd be getting back too late to drive myself home.

Delia's mom answered my knock. When she first opened the door, she just stared. I'd changed my hair in honor of the event. I guess it took her a second to process the information and realize the blond guy on her porch was me.

"Oh, hi, Steve. Come in. Delia's almost ready."

"Thanks." I went inside and walked past Delia's closed door. "Don't rush," I called. "We've got lots of time." I really wasn't worried about being late. It was fine with me if we arrived after the last encore. Down the hall, I heard the doorbell, followed by a quartet of cheerful voices. I wasn't ready to join the crowd, so I stopped to look at the pictures on the wall, trying to kill time by guessing where each one was shot.

I recognized Seaside Heights. And, though I'd never been there, the Eiffel Tower was pretty easy to identify. The picture with the smallmouth bass was probably from one of the large lakes north of here. I thought it was pretty cool that Mr. Kensington had taken Delia fishing. It probably bummed him out that she didn't want to go with him anymore. I had vague memories of fishing with my dad—I couldn't have been more than four or five at the time—but no pictures. I didn't want to dwell on that, so I shifted my attention to other photos.

One shot, with what might have been the Rockies in the background, showed a guy on a Harley. Real biker look—beard, sleeveless denim jacket, boots. Killer tattoo of a two-headed snake on his upper arm. I wondered which side of the family he represented. It would be pretty cool to find out that Delia had a badass uncle stashed somewhere.

Just about the time I'd managed to memorize all the photos, Delia emerged. "Nice outfit," I said. I think she'd just created a new category—erotic preppy. On her, it worked.

"Great spikes," she said, touching my choker.

"Want to wear them?" I asked.

She shook her head. "Not my style."

We joined the other two couples in the living room.

"You know Candace, right?" Delia asked. "And this is Arthur."

I nodded. I'd met Candace a couple times. She was okay, but Arthur looked like he expected me to knife him. Obviously, he didn't know the difference between a punk and a thug. Or maybe he was the sort who expected every person he met to hurt him.

"This is Suzie, and that's Lindon," Delia said.

"Nice," Suzie said, reaching out to touch my hair. "Can I borrow you sometime? I'd love for you to meet my parents."

"I don't think your parents would be amused," Lindon said, grabbing her hand. He gave me his tough-guy look. I gave him my "you're invisible" look.

"Let's hit the road," Delia's dad said. "Traffic's going to get heavy."

When we reached the van, I noticed there were three seats in the back, then two in the middle and two up front. It didn't take a genius to figure out that this wouldn't work well for our trio of couples.

"Would you mind?" Delia asked. "Suzie and Candace are going away next week, so it would be kind of nice if they got to spend as much time as possible with Arthur and Lindon."

"No problem." I went up front. Delia climbed in the back with Arthur and Candace. Suzie and Lindon took the middle.

"To the Dome, driver," I said.

Mr. Kensington touched the brim of an imaginary chauffeur's hat. As he backed out of the garage, he reached for the CD player. "My car, my music," he said.

I braced myself for Verdi, Sinatra, or Conway Twitty. To my relief, what I heard was Clapton. Sure, it was old-folks music, but it was the tolerable sort.

And then there was the less tolerable noise. I discovered, in the alliterative way in which nature sometimes works, that Lindon was a loudmouth.

"Wow, Steve," he said as we headed toward the turnpike, "from behind, you know what your ear looks like with all those rings?"

I shrugged, uninterested in guessing, but glanced back at him to show I could be civilized even around a total dork.

"A shower curtain."

"Clever." I turned away so he could continue to contemplate the back of my head. Apparently, staring wasn't enough for him. He wanted to play with my head, too.

"So, Delia," Lindon said, "I didn't know you'd broken up with Bronk."

"They broke up months ago," Suzie told him. "She dumped him for Ricky Skeffs."

And on they went, discussing an assortment of Delia's old flames. It was a long list. I knew some of the names. Bronk played football for Milton High across the river. Big black guy with dreadlocks and huge biceps. I'd run into him at a party or two. He got along fine with the punk crowd. Skeffs was a skinny loser with a runny nose. Looked strung out most of the time. Most people I knew stayed clear of him. There was even a minor celebrity in the group—Cage Mathus, who drummed for a local metal band. If Lindon was trying to make me jealous, he was wasting his time. Delia's past dates were her business. The present was all that mattered.

But he did get me thinking. It seemed like all of Delia's guys had been handpicked from the set of those most likely to freak out upper-class white parents. No, that couldn't be right. There had to be more to her choices than that. But no other explanation quite fit.

I glanced over at Mr. Kensington as he reached up to adjust the rearview mirror. Beneath the cuff of his short sleeve, I could just see the edge of a tattoo. Snakes, maybe. I stared at his profile and tried to imagine him with a bushy beard. Click. A couple things fell into place. "That's you on the Harley, right?"

"Harley?" He spoke without taking his eyes from the road.

"The photo on the wall. Looks like the Rockies."

"Estes Park." He smiled. "That was a lifetime ago."

"Did you know Mrs. Kensington back then?" I asked.

The smile moved closer to a grin. "Yup. Should have seen the look on her father's face when she brought me home. Thought he was going to pull out a shotgun and chase me off." He laughed and shook his head. "As my wife likes to say, I clean up well."

I glanced over my shoulder, past Lindon and Suzie, at

Delia, who was actively chatting with Candace. I watched her for a while, but she never looked my way.

The traffic grew heavier and then slowed to a crawl when we got near the Dome. We finally reached the parking lot.

"I'll see you kids back here," Mr. Kensington said. "Have fun. I'm going to watch the Phillies and drown my sorrows in club soda." He headed off toward the Hilton.

Delia came over and took my hand. "This is going to be so great."

People stared at us as we made our way to the entrance. I normally didn't pay any attention to that, since it was an everyday thing. But I noticed that Delia scanned the crowd, watching them watch us. Some of them probably didn't see me at all. Delia was quite stunning. But others had that question in their eyes. *What's she doing with him?*

We got to our seats and my stretch of purgatory began. A bad concert is a great place to lose yourself in thought. While Delia and her friends bopped along and screamed and enjoyed the music, I thought about the two of us. It was hard at first to extract actual details. Delia's presence, even in memories, was like a thousand-watt bulb. But I squinted past the gleam and found a string of moments we'd spent together. Fragments. Our first date. We'd been drawn in different directions at the museum. I could have spent all day with the abstracts and surrealists. Delia preferred impressionists.

And after the museum? We went to the movies a couple times, but not to any films I wanted to see. We went to the mall. Delia liked to shop. I didn't. We grabbed a burger or went for coffee, but we didn't talk a whole lot. When we hung out in her room, she'd surf and I'd read.

I was pulled from my thoughts by Delia's words. "It's over," she said.

"What?"

"The concert's over."

"Right."

"You're pretty quiet tonight," she said as we walked back to the parking lot.

I nodded. Hard to know how to respond to that sort of statement. Fortunately, I didn't have to dredge up a reply. All of them started reliving the evening, discussing every song.

"Want me to take the front?" Arthur asked when we reached the van. I guess he figured if he was nice to me I wouldn't stab him.

"That's okay. I don't mind." I climbed into the seat, closed the door, and leaned against the window. Behind me, they kept talking.

Delia was going to a sleepover, so Mr. Kensington dropped her and the girls off first, then took Lindon and Arthur home. I didn't pay any attention to them. I was still wandering through the memories.

"When are you going to do it?" Mr. Kensington asked as he pulled away from Arthur's house.

That jolted me out of my thoughts. "Do what?" Good God, was he asking me if I was going to sleep with his daughter? I wondered whether I should jump from the van before he turned back into a crazed biker and stomped me to death.

"Break up with her," he said.

I let my heart climb back into my rib cage. "How'd you know?" I'd barely accepted it myself.

He shrugged. "Some things are easy to see from a distance. Especially when you've seen them before. Usually, she dumps the guy. Once in a while, it's the other way."

No point lying to him. Or to myself. "You think she'll take it okay?"

He nodded. "Things might get a bit dramatic. And my credit card will take a hit when she shops her way through the pain. But sure, she'll be fine. There's only one thing that worries me."

"What's that?"

"I wonder who she'll bring home next."

There was a moment of silence as I let my imagination play with that question. I figured Mr. Kensington had already dreamed up his own list.

"Why do you think she does it?" I asked.

"Why do you poke holes in your face," he asked me back.

I wasn't sure whether he expected an answer. I wanted to give him one, but I really didn't think I could sum up my life in a sentence or two. Finally, I just said, "That's not the same thing."

He nodded. "Yeah. You're right. It isn't. You're only hurting yourself."

I watched the streetlights pass by outside the window for a couple blocks. Before, at the concert, the breakup was just an idea. It existed in the realm of *Should I?* But now that I'd spoken about it, I knew it was real. *It's over.* I thought about losing Delia. Pictured my existence without her. There was a void, but it wasn't a painful wound. I'd be fine too. It was like if I took out one of my piercings. Eventually, the hole would close up. There might be a small scar, but that was all.

And it wasn't as if I hadn't enjoyed being with her. Whatever her reasons for going out with me, whoever she was trying to shock, we'd had some fun. Maybe, to be honest, I enjoyed the reactions as much as she did. But it was time to move on.

Still, there was something else I didn't want to walk away from. "That lake where you caught the smallmouth . . . ?"

"Manalappa Reservoir," he said. "I belong to a rod and gun club there. It's just an hour north."

"Uh-huh." I felt like a kid at his first dance, tiptoeing around the chance of rejection. "You got any hard feelings against any of her ex guys?"

"Not as long as they treated her right."

I dangled a hint. "Any of them fish?"

"As far as I know, until now, none of them knew a bass from a hole in the ground," he said. "Not that we ever talked much."

"Oh."

We were both quiet for a moment. I realized it had been a stupid idea anyhow.

"You want to go fishing sometime?" he asked.

Or maybe not so stupid. "Yeah. I'd like that."

"Me too."

Then a shadow crossed my mind, cast by an image of the two of us strolling up to the bank, him in khaki with an Eddie Bauer vest, me in black with Ace Hardware chains. "Are you just trying to shock people?" I asked.

We'd reached my place by then. After he pulled to the curb, he turned toward me, a grin on his face. "I hadn't thought of that. But you have to admit, it'll be fun to watch their expressions. Got a lot of good old boys living up that way."

"That could be interesting." I guess he still had a bit of the rebel biker in him. And I guess maybe some of Delia's habits were genetic.

"I'd been thinking of heading out there tomorrow. Join me?"

Did I want to go fishing with my soon-to-be-ex-girlfriend's dad? Life didn't get much weirder than that. "Definitely."

"Pick you up at six?" he asked, holding his hand out, fingers spread, palm facing me.

"Wouldn't miss it," I said, giving him a hand slap. I thanked him for the ride and headed up the walkway, half lost in the past, thinking about the last time I'd felt the tug of a fish on the line.

Then my thoughts shifted to the future. My grin matched his as I imagined what would happen when I told my friends. Maybe even showed them a snapshot of me, Mr. Kensington, and a smallmouth bass. Man, they'd be in for a shock.

PIG LESSONS

BY EDWARD AVERETT

Grandma made me carry a pig around because she caught me with my nose in Jennifer Preston's ear. Let me say first that what she thinks she saw is not what was going on. Don't get me wrong, Jennifer is hot, but she's the kind of girl who would be even hotter if she got rid of the bandanna and the overalls. I should explain that I'm from the city and Grandma lives in the country and Jennifer Preston lives maybe half a mile from Grandma. I wasn't out looking for the girl; she was just used to coming over.

I was at my grandma's because I did something wrong in the city and everybody got fed up with me living there. Some social worker came by and put her big flabby arm around my shoulder and said, "Here's what we're going to do, Jack." Big surprise. It's not like it hasn't happened before.

I tried to explain to her that I didn't really do anything wrong, but she's the kind that shakes her head before you're even done talking. You know, caps you clean before you can even pull the gun out of your waistband.

"But what did I do?"

"You're headed for no good," she said. "They're going to give you one more break. Let you take a breather with your old Grams."

I'm thirteen. I'll never see seventh grade again and those morons think they can still pass me around like a baby? A lot they know. In my house, I was already the man of the family.

Anyway, their new thing is to try to find family instead of strangers to take care of you when the parent thing isn't working out. And since Grandma lost Grandpa a couple of years ago, they thought she might need some man-help around her little farm. She agreed; she's always liked to get back at Mom for my screwups anyway, so they let me out of school early. And here I am.

There's no radio or boom box here. We get to watch Lawrence Welk reruns before lights out at eight. Grandma's banging pots at five in the morning. I think I prefer horns honking and sirens blaring. Even Mom and Deano screaming at each other would have been music to my ears. For the first week I sat up in my rickety little bed with my hands behind my head and wondered what horrible thing I had done to deserve this fate. I couldn't really think of anything and it started getting to be a big bore. So I guess it's no wonder I perked up when Jennifer Preston came to the back door.

"Hi," she said. Real chipper. So naturally I put on The Face. I'm sure you've seen it. It's not a frown, just a mean-bugging kind of look. Don't mess with me, man.

"Are you sick?" she asked.

"What?" That from Grandma, who grabbed my chin and jerked it up so she could look in my eyes.

"Geez," I said, trying to shake away. "Come on."

Grandma kissed my forehead. "No temp," she announced.

Meanwhile, Jennifer's just standing there with a big smirk on her face.

Lesson #1: Girls like to see guys squirm.

Grandma grabbed a pail off the back porch. "Here, Mr. Not Sick Guy, the pigs need watering."

"Did she call yet?" I asked her.

"What do you think?" Grandma said.

I took the pail and headed out the door. I was just about out of hick range when I heard Jennifer say, "Can I come?"

Grandma butted right in. "Of course you can, hon. He's in need of a little company."

Lesson #2: It doesn't matter what age they are, it only takes two females to form a gang.

I walked ahead of her, but she could keep up with words. "Why are your pants that way?" she asked.

I stopped and faced her. "What way?"

"All baggy like that."

"Quit looking at my pants," I said.

"Well, I was just going to say that you're way behind the times if you wear them like that. I mean, I watch *American Idol* and all."

This time I made sure I was walking faster. In no time I was across the yard and ducking through the corral fence. Instead of following me, Jennifer climbed up on the fence and sat watching. I hurried inside the barn.

I was about done filling the pail from the spigot when she showed up. "Don't you have anything better to do?" I asked.

"Plenty."

"Then what are you doing?"

"Hanging with you."

"Hanging with me? Did you say hanging with me?"

"Yeah. Something wrong with that?"

I gave her The Face again and went looking for the pigs. They have a pen on the other side of the barn. It's kind of square and made of metal mesh and the bottom has wooden boards all the way around to keep anything from digging out. There they were; a big sow and eight piglets. When I stepped up on the bottom board to get a better look, they woke up. The little pigs started squealing and the mom stood up and got all protective. Talk about mean. I don't ever want to see eyes like that in a real person. I poured the water into the trough and pretty soon the mom came over and sniffed it with her big snout. There's a life for you. You get to sleep as much as you want. When you're hungry or thirsty, somebody actually comes out and feeds and waters you. You don't have to go looking in the cupboards for something stale to eat. And you don't have to say thanks because you don't know the language.

Jennifer snuck up beside me. "You ever want to be a pig?"

"What? No. Not even."

"I did. When I was little. Till I saw what they do to them."

"What do they do to them?"

"They make them into breakfast. What do you do in the city? Do you like have a posse?"

"A what?"

"You know. Your boys."

Where was she getting this stuff?

I think she could read my mind, because right then, she said, "We've got satellite."

"I've got Rico, Todd, and Jeremy," I said.

"And you stay out late at night and look for trouble in the streets?"

"Yeah, sure," I said.

"And you find trouble or it finds you?"

I nodded. "You got it, sister."

Even though the pig mom was still giving us the evil eye, Jennifer climbed up and sat on the top of the fence. She patted a spot next to her. "Come on."

I put on The Face and sat next to her.

Lesson #3: Girls can cast spells and make you do things you don't want to.

I had to admit she looked better from up close. I saw these freckles on her nose and couldn't keep my eyes off them.

"You like me, don't you?"

"No."

"I can tell you do. Do you have a girlfriend?"

I blew air out and rolled my eyes. "'Course I do."

"I didn't think so. You're not really from the city, are you?"

"You know what? I think I better go back to the house."

But she grabbed my shirt and wouldn't let me go. She had her eyes closed and her lips kind of pooched out. What would you have done? That's what I thought. I leaned over and kissed her. Nice and spongy.

She opened her eyes. "Hmm. Just like I thought," she said. "You'll get better."

"So what's that supposed to mean?"

She jumped down and let out a little whoop. Five minutes before, it would have been really dorky, but now, well, it seemed pretty cool. "Where you going?" I called.

She whooped again and took off. I jumped down and kicked the pail. She was fast, but lucky I caught up with her, just inside the barn door. Or maybe she wasn't that fast or maybe she let me catch up with her. I don't know. My brain was doing jumping jacks. She smiled big and held her face up to me. I kissed her again. Better the second time, by the way.

She nodded. "See what I told you?"

She looked like she was ready for a third, so I moved in on her, but just then, something got her attention. She turned her head, but I kept going, and there I was with my nose in her ear when Grandma stepped into the barn.

I usually wake up about four times before I finally get up in the morning. I kind of drift. It gives me plenty of time to dream. I know I was dreaming about Jennifer some of the time. And about satellite TV a little. But all the time I was on the verge of waking up for good, I kept smelling something weird. Something way out of place. Like a smelly dream. I figured it out when I rolled over and got a good healthy noseful of one of those piglets.

I screamed. The pig squealed. And Grandma let out a cackle that would have put her smack in the chicken category. She was standing at the foot of the bed and watching me kick off the covers and slide off the side. The pig tried to do the same, but its feet were tied together with strips of cloth. It kicked a little and then settled down.

"What the hell?" I said.

"Don't say *hell*," Grandma said. "And don't be sneaking around with any little girl who shows up here."

"I wasn't sneaking," I said.

"You may be right about that."

I stood up and pointed at the pig. "What's that for?"

"He's yours."

"I don't get it."

"Oh, you will, Boy Who Thinks He's a Man. You will."

58

She picked the pig up off the bed and came around and put it in my arms. It looked up at me and I swear it batted its eyelashes.

"And?" I said.

"Consequences," she said. "You go around sticking your nose in a girl's ear, the next thing you know you've got one of those in your arms."

I looked down on it. "A pig?"

"You know what I mean, mister. You're about all I got left in the world. I don't want to have to come up with bail money for another generation of good-for-nothings."

"Grandma, I'm thirteen."

She nodded. "Thirteen and full of snuff and headed down a back road no map'll get you off of."

I laid the pig back on the bed. "I think you have me mixed up with someone else."

"Yeah, maybe I do. I thought you were a kid who had some hope. Now I see you're just like your father."

I hate those words. It wasn't the first time I'd heard them. I don't understand why it is that every time you do something wrong, you're just like your father and whenever you do something right, nobody's saying, Well, that's not a bit like your father. Shouldn't there be credits for doing the right things?

"You don't even know my father," I said.

"I know enough." She picked up the pig again and put it back in my arms. "You take care of him for a while and we'll see how you do."

"How long's a while?"

"A while is a lot less than I had to take care of your mother."

"Doesn't it like need to eat?"

"Yes."

"Who's going to feed it?"

"You are. These piggies are old enough anyway. He'll be fine with you."

"I think it needs its mother."

"We all need our mothers, Jacko. Only maybe not in the same way."

"Has she called yet?" I tried.

Grandma just smiled and pointed at the pig.

"I could just run, you know," I said.

"I know," she agreed. "Just hand me back the pig and say good-bye to your old Grams. Write when you find a place to live."

I looked down at that pig again. "Okay. What does it eat?" I asked.

Lesson #4: No matter what some people think, guys don't have to be pigs.

The first day, me and the pig got to know each other. I had to take the cuffs off because I got really tired of carrying the damn thing around. Two things you need to know about pig-rearing. One, once the cuffs are off, pigs like to run. Two, when they can run, they like to go to the middle of your bedroom floor and do what they do.

"Grandma, he shit on the floor!"

"That's not the place for it," she called back. "And don't say *shit*."

"What do I do with it?"

"If you leave it," she yelled, "you're not going to like it."

I won't even try to explain my first time cleaning up after that pig. Let's just say a porker out of his pigpen is going to have some problems. It's like he couldn't get the feel of it. I'm not kidding, whenever I sat down, he kept nudging up to me in a weird way, like I was his mom or something. If Rico saw that, there'd be no end to the jokes, if you know what I mean.

The bottle thing I got because my mom used one with my baby sister. I asked Grandma about it and she magically came up with one. Pink and plastic. The next day, I was outside on the ground, holding this little guy while he sucked from the bottle and hoping to God no normal person would see me like this, when up walks Jennifer Preston.

"Do you never have anything to do?" I asked.

"I like coming to your crib."

"My crib?"

"Your place."

"I know what crib means."

She sat down next to me and folded up her legs. "It thinks you're its mother," she said.

"I'm not."

"Did its mom die?"

"No."

"So why are you feeding it?"

"Like you don't know."

"Your grandma got pretty mad."

"Yeah, thanks for that."

"What did I do?"

"Acted like a girl. Got me into trouble."

"Is that why you're here?"

I looked at her then. She had that girl look. The "I'm so interested" look. They practice it, you know. In front of the mirror between lunches at school. But that's all it is. Practice. Far as I can tell, they never get it right. I mean-bugged her back.

The pig started kicking then and some of the milk came dribbling out of its mouth.

"Want me to try?" she asked.

Lesson #5: Girls always have a better way of doing things.

She took the pig real careful like. It's a training they go through at girl school. The pig took the bottle and settled right in.

"I think he needs a collar," she said. "And a leash. So he can run around without running away."

That hit me right in the gut for some reason. "Who told you?" I asked.

"Told me what?"

"Did my grandma tell you?"

"Quit wigging out on me, man," she said.

"Well, be careful. I did something really bad. That's why I'm here."

"I figured," she said. "You look a little crazy. Why aren't you in juvey or boot camp?"

"They can't trust me there," I lied.

"Yeah, so that's why they collared you with a pig, because you're so mean?"

"For your information, I have to drag this pig around because of your big ideas."

"I tried to warn you. How did I know you were going to jam me in the ear? You're the big bad boy. You should know better."

"Shut up. I'm sick of your shit." I stood up and grabbed the pig from her. The bottle fell in the dirt. When I hefted him up, he puked all over the front of me.

"You know, it shouldn't be like this," she said.

"Like what?" I was doing my best to clean off the front of me.

"I don't think you should take a baby away from its mom just to teach you a lesson."

"For your information," I said, "my grandma thinks I'm way more important than any damn pig. Besides, it's a weaner."

"A wiener?"

She looked way too freaky. "W-e-a-n-e-r," I spelled out for her. "It means it's ready to be out on its own. Just stay out of it, okay?"

"I will when you tell me what you did."

"It's so bad, I can't tell you."

"So like there was a whole grand jury and everything?"

"Listen, kid, I think you watch way too much satellite TV. Your brain's fried."

"How come all of a sudden you're interested in my brain? If I remember right, it wasn't kissing my brain that got you that foster pig."

"For your information," I tried. "Oh, just forget it, will you?"

"You're a mystery," she said. "I guess I'll just have to wait till they do your biography on A&E."

She walked away then. I noticed she had chucked the coveralls and was wearing a pretty decent pair of jeans.

I thought her idea was good, so I got Grandma to make me up a collar and leash and it worked pretty well.

"You're not getting into any trouble with that guy, are you?" she asked.

"What trouble can you get into with a pig?" I asked back.

"You'd be surprised," she said.

This time I looked at her and raised my eyebrows. But Grandma shook her head. "Not yet," she said.

I went back out and walked the damn pig through the barn and over to his old pen. That wasn't a bright idea. He got all squealy and yanked at the leash. I started laughing because it looks pretty funny to have a baby pig with his ears pinned down trying to run while you're holding him back. His little hooves were just digging into the ground. But the really funny part was what the mom pig was doing. I mean, she started snorting like, well, a pig. She put her big old pink snout up against the wood slat of the fence and tried pushing it through. I would swear she was gnawing on the damn thing. The piglet would squeal and the mom would snort and stamp, like they meant something to each other. All the other piglets put their little noses through the boards and started squealing too. A whole family of snorters and squealers. It should make you fall down and laugh. But it didn't.

I was so glad Jennifer wasn't out there because then I would have ruined all her illusions about me. Seeing that little pig family straining so hard to get to the lost boy, well, it made me cry a little.

Lesson #6: Crying alone can only make you lonely.

I sat down on my butt and dragged the piglet over to me and put him on my lap. He was still wailing and his mom was a whole mess of snort, but I think he liked having my hands around him. Seeing him like that, I forgave him for doing it on my bedroom floor.

By the end of the second day, I was tired of dragging him around, but Grandma would have none of letting me off the hook.

"I don't know why I've got to do this," I said. "I haven't done nothing."

"I saw what I saw," she said. "You calling me a liar?"

"No," I admitted. "Only it wasn't my fault."

"Oh, and I suppose that little girl is to blame. After all she's been through, you're going to tack on taking responsibility for you."

"What's she been through?"

"I guess you would like to know, wouldn't you? For your information, you couldn't put up with what she's gone through. At least your mother is still breathing air. Not that she much appreciates the oxygen."

"She doesn't have a mother?"

"No, and don't go blabbing it around to her. It was the cancer, plain and simple. It happens to the best of us. Don't be thinking it was anything that girl did. By the way, your kid's dribbling."

I felt the front of my shirt grow warm. I would never be able to wear it again. "Did my mom?" I asked.

"Again you ask me? I was young and good-looking the last time she called me. You're not expecting her to, are you?"

"No. Just wondering. Does she have a dad?"

"Who? Your ma?"

"No, Jennifer."

"Yeah, you could call him that. He's a busy man, that one. Too busy to raise kids. Busy on the farm. Busy at the local bar. You going to clean that shirt, or am I going to choke to death from pig fumes?"

I couldn't sleep very well that night. I made a cool diaper out of a dishtowel and I kind of liked putting it on the pig. He looked up at me with big old dark eyes and I think he appreciated me doing it. It reminded me of my little sister, how giggly she got when I changed her diaper.

Lesson #7: A kid shouldn't have to take care of another kid. But he can do a good job anyway.

I think Grandma thought I did something wrong and maybe I did, but sometimes you have to do what's best. I didn't actually steal my little sister. But try telling that to anybody. You know when it's not safe. You just know. No matter what your mom says, you know. Or that social worker. I'd do it again too. Only I didn't tell her that.

I woke up early because the pig was squealing. Kind of like a cry. I couldn't take it anymore. Downstairs, Grandma was banging the pots. "You're getting used to our time, aren't you?"

I took my pig and walked to Jennifer's house. Even though it was early, she was sitting on the front steps with a herd of cats all around her. They all ran when they saw the pig.

"What are you doing here?" she asked.

I held the pig out. "I can't get him to shut up. What are you doing?"

"Waiting for my dad."

"He left already?"

"No. He hasn't come back."

"You don't have to tell me," I said.

"I know. But I made a decision and I've got to tell you. I don't really have satellite. I hear about it from girls at school. We only get three channels, unless the wind is blowing, then we only get one and it's fuzzy. And you're the first boy I ever kissed."

Lesson #8: Girls like to talk.

"And I have an older sister and she used to take care of me but she got married and lives too far away, but someday I'll get to visit her. She calls me once a week, but it used to be twice only she and her husband are on a budget, so she had to cut it down to one or maybe every two weeks, but I understand."

She looked at me then, like we had some kind of pact. It made me nervous, so I pushed the pig in her face. "I can't get him to stop crying. What should I do?"

"I think we should put him back."

"My grandma will kill me. I haven't learned my lesson yet."

"What lesson?"

"I don't know."

She ended up coming with me. She even carried the pig when he got tired. Back at the farm, I could see Grandma in the kitchen through the window.

"She's nice," Jennifer said. "She calls me all the time to make sure I'm okay."

"Let's go," I said.

Pretty soon, we were at the pigpen. The big sow was lying on her side sleeping and the little ones were piled on top of each other.

"What if she doesn't take him back?" I said.

"Sure she will. Moms always take their kids back."

"Not always," I said.

By this time, the piglet was putting up a fuss again and waking up the whole brood. They got up against the fence just like the last time and let me know they meant business.

"Kind of funny," I said.

"What is?"

"You ever seen a family get like this?"

"My mom was that way," she said.

"I know about her," I said.

Lesson #9: Boys like to talk too. Only they don't always know it.

It just flowed out of me. "I caught my mom in the bathroom again with Deano, who is not my dad by the way, and they were sitting all spread-eagle against the tub with the lighter and the spoon and I just couldn't take my little sister crying in her own piss anymore so I snatched her and took her away. And I ran till I didn't recognize my neighborhood anymore and I found a good place and I went inside and the first lady I saw, I handed her my sister and then I ran back out and never looked back. Only they caught me and all hell broke loose and we all got sent away. I don't know where my sister is now."

"You don't have to tell me," she said.

"I know. I don't come from any smart-ass place. I don't have any friends who roam the streets looking for fun or drugs or girls. I stay home at night and try to do my homework and I'm afraid to go out. And my grandma's my last chance because I never can stand it when they put me other places."

"Well . . ."

"And you're the first girl I ever kissed. But I did get slapped once for almost kissing a girl."

Jennifer walked over and started taking off the pig's collar. "Damn," she said. "I thought maybe you'd be so cool, you could teach me to dance."

"Really?"

"No. There. Now he's free."

I held the squirming pig for a second. It was weird. He knew where he wanted to be. I was pretty sure we all wanted to be there.

"You want me to do it?" Jennifer asked.

"No, I'd better do it." I climbed the fence, which

caused a whole new ruckus down below. If pigs could jump, I'd be dead now. It's hard to hang on to a squirmy little thing with one hand, but I gave it my best shot. I had it lowered pretty far down before it rolled out of my hand and hit the ground with a thump. Jennifer jumped up next to me. The mother pig had her snout down like she thought the little guy was dinner. The other pigs kind of trampled all over him for a while. I thought for a second that if you've been gone too long, they might forget you, but instead of eating him, the mother nudged him back up on his feet. He shook his whole body for a second and then ran for the pig pile.

Lesson #10: You usually end up where you belong.

Back at the house, Grandma met us at the door. "Well, what do you know," she said. "It's Mr. Once Had a Pig and Now He Doesn't."

"What about me?" Jennifer asked.

"Well, you, Miss Used to Have Good Taste and Now She Has None. What can I say? You two want breakfast?"

"She's never going to call, is she?" I asked.

Grandma took a second and I saw the spatula in her hand shake a couple of times, but she's a tough old bird. I like that in a grandma. "No, darling, she's not going to."

"Okay," I said. "That's it then. Are we eating?"

"Are you cooking?" Grandma asked.

"I'm the kid," I protested.

"I know," she said.

"And no bacon, please," I said.

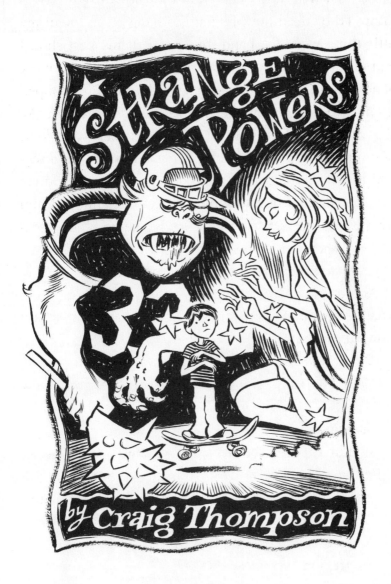

Looking back, our only truly nerdy attribute was that we LONGED to be like the "cool" guys.

HOOL PRIDE

We were jealous and subservient to the alpha males, and thus constantly PERSECUTED.

ONCE WE LET GO OF THESE INSECURITIES, WE WERE EMPOWERED--

PUNK ROCK!

The envy we once had for your lives has been replaced by PITY!

Yup, we're COOLER than you.

We are violating your mores deliberately to provoke you!

THE UNBEATABLE

BY MO WILLEMS

Near invincibility sucks.

Everybody's dying to figure out your one weakness so they can kick your butt and become top of the heap. That means between 8:30 A.M. and 3:00 P.M. I spend my weekdays getting ultra-dense carbonic-acidium sprayed in my eyes at extra-sonic speeds, being struck by the mythic *Lightning of Thardorferd*, or blasted by gamma-pain rays, semi-nuke projectiles, and titanium poison darts by my classmates. Once, the class clown, who goes by the blindingly original name *The Class Clown*, even tried to give me a wedgie.

Welcome to my school: *NewMan Academy for the Enhanced*, better known on the streets as Sky High (on account of our campus hovering nine thousand feet above Manhattan). Sky High was founded fifty years ago, after "The Alien Scourge" nearly ate Europe. The school's mission: Teach the earth's one hundred most super-powered kids readin', writin', and world-savin'. I'll tell you what, standards must have been higher during the "Golden Age," because most of my peers will be lucky if they can get work as underwear models after graduation. Oh, did I mention our mandatory school uniforms, with the little green capes, big green *N*'s on the chest, and BVDs on the outside of our tights? They suck too.

I'm Bill Blaze, better known to the rescued population as *The Unbeatable*. Yeah, the name's totally lame, but it's not like I had a choice when *The Mystic Spirit of Ancient Wisdom* (who goes by Mike for short) appeared in my bedroom when I was a fourteen-year-old happy, normal, un-super kid. I open my closet and suddenly, the room is all lit up and this Mike guy announces I've inherited *The Mantle of the Wise* and transforms me into the most powerful, indestructible being on the planet with the stupidest name ever. I suggested *Sir Righteous, the Butt-Kicker Supreme* as an alternative, but Mike was not receptive.

So, *ka*-whoosh! I'm packed off to Sky High, where the forty-foot-tall *Invincible Principal* drags me into the assembly hall and announces in front of ninety-nine ambitious, super-powered future classmates that I'm the best of the best, strongest of the strongest, A-Number One, a shoo-in for *The Guild of Heroes*, blah, blah, blah . . . He might as well have painted a target on my back while he was at it, because everyone in the hall was seething (the class president, *Loco-Motion*, literally had smoke streaming out of her mechanical ears). Great first day, huh?

Hey, I'd be jealous of me too, if I was some mid-powered freak hoping to break out from under his or her Super-Parents' shadow. We've got *The Electric Boogaloo*'s daughter, who just wants to be a veterinarian when she grows up, not *Electric Boogaloo Two, Possessor of the Super-Sonic Disc of Disco*. But Daddy got her into Sky High and he's going to make sure she graduates top of the class whether she likes it or not. Then there are those blue-blooded kids whose families have been in the hero biz for so many generations, their powers have diluted into nothing, like *Diz-Comfort*, the guy who can barely even make others itchy. These are not happy people, and they don't like being reminded of all they "should" be by the new kid who just won the power lottery.

That's not to say it's all bad being number one in the powers department. My X-ray vision was a welcome diversion until they installed lead walls in the girls' showers. And I'm in the same homeroom as the infamous *Super-Model, Miss X*. Believe me, it's not her brain pulsars that make her victims weak in the knees.

Well, it's been a few years and my life's settled into a dull, violent routine: In the morning a few (of the stupider) underclassmen try to ambush me with their fire-, or ice-, or rubber-band-, or whatever-powers before I get to my locker, which is usually booby-trapped with an interdimensional-destructo-field, followed by the popular clique called *The Never Minds* clumped together and staring at me with their third eyes from across the hall as they try to reach into my subconscious to get the latest gossip and fry my brain. Oh, let's not forget the obligatory group tackle from *Brick Face and Stucco*, the tough guys from the burbs whose impenetrable skin (or "siding") was invented by some Mobbed-up Mad Scientist. By the time I'm halfway to my *Physics of the Inverse Universe* class, that little four-foot-tall half-brat, half-mecha hybrid from Detroit, *Motor Mouth*, skids up next to me with his hydraulic 900-horsepower jaw and stammers, "So-what's-your-weakness? Huh? What-is-it? Huh? Huh? Huh? Huh? Huh? Huh?"

"Don't got one, gas-breath."

"Everybody's-got-a-weakness!" The little turd smiles, flashing his spark-plug grin. "That-exchange-student-*Das-Goth*'s-skin-burns-in-bright-light.*The-Eagle*-molts-on-the-winter-solstice. *The-Bee*'s-got-terrible-hay-fever . . ."

"And all those guys suffered near-fatal attacks as soon as their secrets got out," I snarl.

"I'll-find-out-anyway-Un-Beat-a-Billy," he continues at 95 miles an hour. "Why-don't-we-just-save-some-time-tell-me-yours-and-I'll-tell-ya-mine."

"I already know your weakness," I reply as I turn down the hall. "You're an asshole."

"HOW-COME-YA-NEVER-FIGHT-BACK-BILLY!?" he calls loud enough for everyone to stop and look at me. "YA-TOO-GOOD-TO-FIGHT-LIKE-THE-REST-OF-US!?

YA-GOT-SOME-INCREDIBLE-POWER-TO-BROWN-
NOSE-WE-DON'T-KNOW-ABOUT?"

I stop and glance back at *Motor Mouth* before chirping, "I promised your momma I wouldn't bust you up and sell you for scrap this semester."

That heats his engine good, but at least it shuts him up like I hoped. It's unwise to remind everyone that I don't fight back. As it is, I get stabbed in the back more often than I would if I occasionally punched a few freshmen through a wall or something. Too bad this school is filled with ninety-eight selfish bastards like *Motor Mouth*, and only has one Rose.

Rose. God, I can't even figure out what she's doing here, she's so nice and smart and . . .

I remember this one time, *Hot-Head*'s in the cafeteria, her face flaming bright and yelling, "What are you supposed to do!?" Rose just stands there as the ends of her hairs are being singed off and smiles and says, "I guess I'm here to make you look good, but that's not working." It was like a bucket of water from nowhere. *Hot-Head* looked so stupid, she just flamed down and flew out of there.

I flash on that moment while some sophomore called *Four Eyes* tries to impress his girlfriend by blasting me with ocular laser fire. Then Rose walks up and starts talking to me. Now, we've talked before, but mostly Rose does what the others do; she avoids me. Seriously, who wants to hang with someone who's constantly being shot at?

"Hey," she says like *hey* is the most important word in the world and only she knows how to pronounce it.

"Hey." I'm kind of distracted. I don't know if she's impervious to laser fire, so I want to make sure to deflect all the laser blasts before they can incinerate her.

"I . . . I've got this, uh, project. About 'Speed of Light Travel' or somethin'. So, I was wondering, y'know, if you could help me out, uh, somewhere with less distractions."

I'm so surprised that she's (kinda) asking me out, I let a blast zip by that blows *The Loser*'s locker into a fireball of burning notebooks for the third time this week. Trying to regain my cool, I stammer, "The moon's pretty quiet." I don't have to be a mind reader to see in her eyes that she's never been out of the atmosphere. I never thought to ask if she's space-capable! Smooth move, Super Dork.

But after she thinks about it for a second, Rose mutters totally matter-of-factly, "Cool. Eight o'clock, 'kay?" She flashes this small, intense smile before she turns and walks away. Those grins definitely have to be one of her powers.

Okay, I'm gonna take back what I said about my life totally sucking before.

There's this common misconception that all super-heroes get some sort of kick out of dressing up like clowns on steroids. We don't. If you've ever worn a cape for Halloween, you have an inkling how uncomfortable we are while we're battling evil. I, for one, prefer blue jeans and a wool sweater over a T-shirt, but I wear my costume to battles so that the Bad Guys (who by the way, really do like dressing up) can see me better. If I'm easy to spot, then the villains will probably shoot at me instead of innocent civilians. It's simple Villain Psychology 101. That being said, there are some kids at school who totally wear masks to hide their acne.

So, I get to the moon like an hour or so early to case out the crater I told Rose about. I know, I know, paranoid. But you can't ever let your guard down. I've been surprised enough times by villains and underclassmen, and I don't want a potentially romantic evening to be interrupted by some embarrassing thermo-nuclear attack. The place is clean; no freeze-traps or brain-sucking microbes, just a big, quiet, peaceful world floating through space at a weary distance from earth. I spot some golf balls and a club left by the astronauts in the '70s and take a couple of practice shots (my golf coach, always afraid that I'll whack a ball into orbit, tells me, "Others can give it 110 percent. Do me a favor and give it 12 percent"). I wait for Rose.

She beams in wearing sweats and slippers and her smile. You'd think she'd be sexier in her skintight school uniform, but right now, she looks perfect.

It takes me a second to remember I'm supposed to be here helping her with her "project."

We talk about near light-speed travel, about how galactic dust always gets caught in your teeth, and how when you approach Ultimate Velocity, you start losing weight from your hips and thighs (which is why *The Cheerleader Squad* spend all their free time zipping around the galaxy). She asks me what it's like when you go fast enough for time to stand still and I tell her it's like sitting on the moon with her.

She smiles her smile, closes her notebook, and starts talking about herself.

The way she explains it, Rose's powers seems to be, well, limitless. She's somehow been befriended by a squad of *Guardian Angels* that she trusts to grant her whatever abilities she needs in the moment. She wasn't sure she'd survive the cold vacuum of space, but she hoped her *Guardians* would help out and bravely beamed onto the moon. That's pretty cool.

Then Rose does what no one has ever done before: She tells me her weakness. "I have to take any challenge I'm given," she explains almost sadly. "Or I'll lose my powers forever."

"You mean, if you say no just once, you go back to being like mortal and all?" I ask.

She smiles a new smile, one that's exhausted and exhilarated at the same time.

"You shouldn't have told me that," I finally say. "I could ruin your life with knowledge like that."

"Others have. But you won't." How many different smiles does that girl have? Each one is more compelling than the last.

". . . I don't fight back because it hurts."

Did I just say that? Out loud? Stupid. Dumb. Weak.

91

But Rose gives me a quiet look and I feel, I dunno, could it be that I feel . . . relieved? Well, that's it, everything I've bottled up, every secret I've kept since I got these terrible, awesome powers dumped on me two years ago, spills, just pours out.

"I feel whatever pain I inflict," I blurt out quickly. "If I punch somebody in the face, my jaw feels like it's splintering into a million pieces. If I ever killed some-one, I'd die. That's why I never fight back. I'm . . . I guess I'm afraid of the pain. But with all my power, it's not easy holding back. So many times I want to just, like, kick the crap out of everyone. I always feel like I'm an inch away from really hurting myself. Heh, and others too, I guess.

"It sucks, but when Mike, the 'wise' being that gave me my powers (without asking me, by the way) put this restriction on me, he called it my 'learner's permit,' and told me that I'll get my full 'license' when I was 'ready.' *Ready*? When's that? It's like I have to pass some big test, but no one will tell me what or when it is! Anyway, it just sucks."

Rose looks at me like she's about to cry, which is not exactly what you're supposed to make a girl do on the first date. Then she grabs hold of my hand and we scan the sky for exploding stars.

It's a cold night as I fly back to the dorm, but I don't feel it.

Someone left the light on in the bathroom, but it's not

my roommate, *Excelsior*. (I can hear him watching a sci-fi marathon in the living room.) Slowly, silently, I hover down the hall. Before opening the door I mutter, "Hey, Mike."

"That's *The Mystic Spirit of Ancient Wisdom* to you, squirt," replies the ghostly, floating, bearded vision, an accumulation of wisdom spanning three eons and five continents in wispy form. "I'm on official business."

"You gonna give my cat superpowers too?" I ask, testily. "'Cuz if you are, maybe you can stop him from peeing all over my bed while you're at it."

"Very funny," remarks the ghost just before the room is bathed in *Pure Light* and his voice echoes with the *Truth of Time*.

"WILLIAM BLAZER. THE 'RESTRICTION' IS LIFTED. THOU MAY SMITE WITHOUT FEAR OF PAIN. THOU MAY DESTROY WITHOUT BEING DESTROYED. THOU ART INVINCIBLE AND FREE. USE THINE POWER WISELY."

As light fades and my eyes adjust, Mike adds in his best mock spokesman voice, "This decision was brought to you by *The Seven Hot Shots of Eternal Wisdom*. '*Eternal Wisdom*: Now more than ever!'"

"Why'd you let me off the hook now?" I ask seriously. "Because I told someone about my weakness? Was that the 'test'?"

"You told someone?" remarks Mike, floating before me with a knowing smirk. "Well, that's none of my beeswax. And just 'cuz you got your license, don't think you graduated yet." As Mike fades into the air, he sticks out his tongue at me. For an ancient mystic spirit, he has some serious maturity issues.

I brush my teeth and go to bed.

So, I wake up smiling and I'm all, Underclassmen better not mess with *The Unbeatable* today, because my boss opened me up a big can of whoop-ass last night and I'm ready for a taste! Oh, and I think I got me a girlfriend to boot, so all's good on planet Bill.

Strange thing is, there's no one in the locker room to pester me. In fact, the halls are deserted. Then I fly out to the quad: It's packed with, like, half the school or something. Did I forget a pep rally?

Then I see that eight-piston jaw grinning in the middle of the crowd. It's *Motor Mouth.* His engine is revving, his palms are sweating, his squinty eyes shiny like headlamps; this turd is happier than I've ever seen him.

"WE-KNOW, HURTY-BOY! WE-GOT-YOUR-WEAK-NESS-DOWN! TOLD-YOU-I'D-FIND-OUT!" Motor Mouth screams, carefully pronouncing every word so that his crowd of bullies won't miss a beat. "NOW-ME-AND MY-BUDDIES-ARE-GONNA-MAKE-YOU-FIGHT! WE'RE-GONNA-MAKE-YOU-BREAK-YOUR-ARMS TWENTY-TIMES-OVER! WE'RE-GONNA-MAKE-YOU PUNCTURE-YOUR-LUNGS! WE'RE-GONNA-PUNK-YOU OUT! YOU'RE-GONNA-HURT, OH-BABY-YOU'RE-GONNA HUUUURT!"

"Are you auditioning for the school play?" I sneer while I try to figure a way out of this. "Seriously. 'You're gonna huuuurt!' What is that? Next thing you're going to tell me that this time it's personal."

"JUST-GET-HIM!" *MM* screeches like a crazy person. The crowd powers up. This is going to get ugly. People are going to get hurt.

The whole quad hums with enough power to level an entire city. I've never seen so many hungry looks. The fliers hover upward.

I try to remain calm as I snarl, "Uh, just a quick word to all my would-be attackers. Last night my pal *The Mystic Spirit of Ancient Wisdom* (perhaps you've heard of him) visited me in my bathroom and lifted the 'restriction' *Motor Mouth* so kindly informed you about. So I'm free to kick your butts deep into another eon without any negative side effects."

The mob becomes uneasy. Who wants to get the crap kicked out of them if it's not going to help take me down?

"HE'S LYING!" bellows *Motor Mouth*, foaming oil at the mouth. Seriously, this guy's got to take some acting lessons or watch better movies.

"Maybe. Maybe not," I reply calmly as my body starts to glow red with *Unbeatable Power*. Electric sparks shoot out of my body. My eyes glow golden. I'm a fearsome sight as I say quietly, but seriously, "Now, who wants to be the first to find out?"

There aren't that many gamblers in the mob, so it doesn't take too long for the crowd to melt away. The moment is over without a punch thrown. Pretty soon even *Motor Mouth* slinks away, fuming but silent.

All that is left is Rose. And suddenly, I get it.

I ask the question, hoping, praying, needing her to say no; desperate for her to tell me that it was a coincidence. "*Motor Mouth* put you up to going out with me last night just so you could weasel out the secret?"

She's got a new smile on, and it's not pretty. "I had to accept the challenge, Bill," she says softly and honestly. "I explained that."

In a nanosecond, I zoom forward in a blind rage, grab her face in my hand, and yell, "Hope your *Guardian Angels* know their stuff," before I fling her body across the quad and through the Mask-Making and Crafts Building. Forty thousand pounds of brick collapse onto her.

I don't feel a thing. Except shame.

PRINCES

BY DAVID LEVITHAN

The minute I hit high school, the minute the train station was only a walk away, I escaped into the city and danced. I had been practicing since I was seven—practicing to be that kind of body, the kind that gets away. Right after school, two days a week. Then three. Then four. The *Nutcracker* in winter, the big recital right before summer. I outgrew my teacher and his storefront studio. Cut class to audition for a modern dance studio in Manhattan. Treated my acceptance like the keys to the city.

When you're a boy dancer, your progression through the *Nutcracker* is like this: First you're a mouse, then you're a Spaniard, then you're a prince. I could feel my body changing that way, from something cute and playful to something strange and foreign, then finally something approaching beauty. You start off wanting to be a snowflake, to be a character. But then you realize you can be the movement itself.

I loved watching the boys, and I loved being the boy who was watched. Not as a mouse, not as a Spaniard. But now, as a prince.

I doubt my parents knew what they were getting into when they let me go to that first dance class. I know some fathers justify it by saying it will help when the boy grows up to be a quarterback, when he has to dance past the linebackers. I know some mothers tell other mothers that it's so much better than staying on the couch all day. My parents never really discussed the subject with me. They came to the *Nutcracker*s, they came to the big recitals, and they came to the conclusion that I was gay. Not every boy who dances is gay, or grows up to be gay. But come on. A whole lot of us are.

My parents and I never talked about it. They didn't stop showing up, so I took that as acceptance.

My brother, Jeremy, came to most of the performances too. When he was five and I was ten, he got all worried that our Jewish family was starting to celebrate Christmas, with all of the red, green, and white costuming going on. It was only when he realized he was celebrating me instead of celebrating Santa that he was all for it. Five years younger than me, always a kid in my eyes. Whether he knew I was gay or not didn't really matter to me. He wasn't going to be a part of that part of my life.

That part resided in the city. Specific address: the

Broadway studios of the Modern Dance Workshop, housed in a rent-by-the-hour space between Prince and Spring in SoHo, with a view of a publishing company across the street. I had to audition four times in order to get in—there were only twenty students, mostly city, some suburban. Six guys, fourteen girls. The instructors were either older dancers who'd been worn down into choreographers, or aspiring dancers looking for a day job to support their auditioning habits. There was Federica Rich, a middle-aged footnote of the footlights. There was quiet, unassuming Markus Constantine, who looked at us not so much as teenagers but as potential trajectories, mapping the mathematics of our every movement. His counterpoint was Elaine, who'd just graduated from the dance program at Michigan and clearly belonged to the dance-as-therapy school. She was always examining her reflection in our wall of mirrors.

And Graham. At twenty-two, he was only five years older than me. He hadn't gone to college; he'd danced his way across Europe instead. He was beautiful in the way that a breeze is beautiful—the kind of beauty you feel gratitude for. From the minute I saw him behind the table at my fourth audition, I knew I would be dancing for him. To make him watch, so I could return the watching.

I was not the only one. We'd all tell stories about Graham and treat them like facts, or glean small facts and turn them into stories. Carmela had heard that he'd been an underwear model in Belgium. Tracy said he once dated one of the male leads at Tharp, and that when he'd left, the lead had drunk himself into a depression. Eve said this wasn't true; the dancer had been from Cunningham, not Tharp.

I wanted to be the one to find out the truth. I wanted to become a part of the truth, part of the story.

Mostly, I hung out with the girls. They weren't competition. As for the other boys—only one or two were a real threat. Connor had the inside track with the teachers, since he'd been at MDW for two semesters now. Phillipe was much stronger than he was graceful, but he was also named Phillipe, which I had to imagine gave him an advantage. As for the others—everyone trusted that Thomas had been accepted because of his trust fund; Miles seemed intimidated by the sound of his own footsteps; and George leaped like a gazelle but landed like a lumberjack. Modern dance is forgiving of many things, but it still discriminates against the balance-impaired.

From the minute I got on the train, I felt I was already in the city, already a part of that rush. But when I got into the studio, the city ceased to be anything but a traffic buzz in the background. That room contained a world.

On the train ride back, I would try to hold on to it. I would replay Graham's single nod to me a hundred times over, watching it from every angle. If he said anything to me, I would gather the sentences like a shell seeker. Sitting on the orange reversible seats, jutted back and forth by the rhythm of the rails, I would try to remember all of my movements. Inevitably, the ones that came back the most were the errors—the slight wobble of the ankle, the unfortunate and unintended dip of the arms. My memory became slave to the corrections I would need to make. More so if Graham had noticed.

I could have called one of my parents to pick me up when I got into the station, but I was never ready to see them, never ready to concede that I was home so soon. So I walked the mile home. My body, having just been sitting for a half hour, reawakened to a new kind of fatigue—not the adrenaline exhaustion of having just finished, but the unoiled hinges of afterward, when everything catches up with you and your body lets you know how it truly feels. Sometimes I loved that ache, because it felt like an accomplishment. Other times I was tired of everything.

I always stayed until the last possible moment of class, and then sometimes a few of the girls and I would run to Dojo for a yogurt shake or a cheeseburger. By the time I got to my street, suburbia was empty of cars, of noise, of movement. Even the reading light in Jeremy's room was off, the new chapter dog-eared for the night. My parents' room emanated a blue television glow; if I went close to the window, I could hear the sound of *Law & Order* suspects being caught, or the roll call of the news. By the time I passed their doorway, my parents were usually asleep, even if the television wasn't.

I was seventeen, halfway toward eighteen, and I had learned something nobody had ever taught me: Once you get to a certain age, especially if a driver's license is involved, you can go a whole day—a whole week, even—

without ever seeing your family. You can maybe say good morning and maybe say good night, but everything in the middle can be left blank.

I saw Jeremy a few minutes every morning at breakfast. He was just starting to really grow, almost thirteen. His awkward voice didn't faze me, but the way his body was beanstalking, beginning to fit into itself, was strange. I knew there were probably things I should be telling him—but then I figured that I'd pieced it together without the help of an older brother. I wanted him to be independent. So I left him alone.

Did I know him at all? Yes. He was class president material, in a town where that was more a measure of affability than popularity. He would grow up to be the boy every girl's parents wanted her to bring home. He was ingratiating without being grating. He was, I imagined, an okay guy.

And did he know me at all? He knew me as the brother who was always leaving. So maybe the answer was yes.

One of the reasons I was so happy to avoid my house was that everyone else was deeply involved in the preparations for Jeremy's Bar Mitzvah. My own Bar Mitzvah had been stressful enough—forget coming of age, it was more like a see-how-many-times-his-voice-can-crack contest. (The answer: roughly 412 times in one morning service.) The experience left me with a sheaf of savings bonds and little else. Jeremy's, if anything, was going to be more elaborate. Jeremy seemed less bothered by this than I was. He deferred everything but the Torah portion to our parents, and appeared grateful and interested when things such as appetizers and candle color were discussed. After my recommendation for a bacon-flavored cake, I wasn't consulted.

Two more weeks. I only had two more weeks to put up with the preparations. My mother had made me pick out my tie over a month ago. I was set.

At class, we didn't acknowledge our parents. No, that's not true—we were willing to acknowledge their faults. I kept relatively quiet during these conversations, because I had less to check off on the dishonor roll of slights and abuses. Carmela's dad had left and her mom had given up. Eve's stepmother nearly broke Eve's leg. Miles's parents were in a constant state of disowning him. Although he'd never say it, we knew he was working two jobs to pay for tuition. Every now and then Thomas, our trust funder, would strip a twenty from his parents' billfold and we would all draw hearts on it before slipping it into Miles's gym bag.

Graham never talked about his parents or where he'd come from. When he said "home," he meant his basement apartment in the East Village. I imagined it so clearly, down to the rag rug on the floor and the incense holder on the bedside table. Sometimes I would play an infinite game of Twenty Questions with him, trying to use each question to narrow him down even further, to get to his one single answer. Did he live alone? Yes, if you didn't count the uninvited mouse. Was he happy in New York? Yes, but in a different way than he'd been happy in

Barcelona or Paris. What did he think of *Center Stage*? That God was cruel to make Ethan Stieffel straight.

From the way he criticized my dancing, I knew he thought I had a chance. You don't need to go to too many classes to know the difference between a teacher who points out your errors because they are beyond help and need to be pointed out as an obligation to dance itself, and the instructors who tear you down because they think you can rebuild in the proper way. Graham didn't hold back his corrections, but he didn't hold back his praise either.

We each had to perform in a piece, and Graham chose me to be in his. While Elaine dangled her dancers in Debussy, Markus knit together swathes of Schubert, and Federica fastened on to flamenco, Graham decided to make a suite out of recent Blur songs. *An aria of dislocated longing,* he called it. *A dance for the anonymously lovelorn,* I answered. He nodded, happy with me.

Practice was different now. He would touch me, guide me, manipulate me into the right contours, the shape of his vision. I was used to this, but not in this way. This was not the *Nutcracker*. This was personal. I was prince now of a kingdom that was still being defined.

There was a movement I couldn't get. A turn with arms outstretched. I could not get my arms to match his direction—or maybe it was that he could not get his direction to match with words. My arms spread too much like wings, then too much like broken branches. They embraced too much of the air, then they did not hold the space tight enough. Graham came behind me and mapped my arms with his, held my hands and made every point align, wrist to shoulder. I closed my eyes, taking in the angles, the arcs, his breathing against my neck. When he let go, I stayed in the pose. *David's slingshot*, he called it, and I knew I wouldn't get it wrong again.

When we were done, he asked me to join him for a drink. I knew it wasn't a date. I knew he wasn't asking me out. But what my mind knew, my hope ignored. It was my hope that was disappointed when I came out of the changing room to find a whole entourage waiting for me. It was my hope that faltered when Carmela said, "Are you coming or not?"

But my hope was stubborn. When Graham held back so we'd be side by side on the sidewalk, my hope ignored everything else and held on to the single fact of his proximity, his choice. He led us from the back, calling out directions to George and Carmela until we made it to Beauty Bar, which used to be a beauty parlor but now served cocktails. The décor was still Retro Beautician, with half-dome hair dryers attached to the backs of many of the chairs. There were six of us, and Graham was the only one who was legal. We gave him money and he represented us at the bar, returning with Cosmopolitans stemmed through his fingers, perfectly balanced.

He chose to sit next to me and then he chose to talk to me for the next hour. We talked about Paris, and I tried to erase my family from as much of our family vacation as I could. He touched my arm for emphasis and left it there. Our legs came into perfect contact. He glinted at me.

Is this really happening? I thought. Then I saw Miles on the other side of Graham. Noticing. He smiled at me, as if to say, *Yes, it is happening.*

I didn't feel that many steps younger than him. He wasn't treating me that way. If I didn't feel like his equal, then at least I felt like he was welcoming me into the range.

I wanted every word to last for hours, every gaze to last for days. I wanted to confiscate all our watches, banish all the clocks. But inevitably Graham looked down at his wrist and realized there was somewhere else he needed to be. There was no question, no discussion, that the rest of us would go when he did. Staying would be like trying to act out the trick after the magician had left the stage.

Graham hugged us all good-bye. My hug lasted a little longer, had a little tighter squeeze at the end.

I wanted to kiss him. I wanted him to want to kiss me.

But not on the street corner, not with George and Miles and Carmela and Eve there. We all dispersed, me and Miles walking together to the subway. I was practically floating—and then I realized that Miles, in his quiet way, was floating too.

"Wasn't that amazing?" he asked. "I mean, that place. And that drink. And everything. I can't wait for life to be like that, can you?"

No, I told him. I couldn't wait.

I wasn't planning on waiting.

When it was time for us to part, he opened his arms for an embrace. I figured this was now the way we would all say good-bye.

As he hugged me, Miles said, "You're pretty cool, you know."

"You're drunk," I told him.

He pulled back with a smile and said, "In a way." Then he said good night again and disappeared with a wave.

On the train ride home, I wondered if I should have asked for Graham's phone number, what it would be like to hear his voice at midnight, the last sound before going to sleep. It was late when I got home, but not too late. Still, my father was waiting for me when I came into the kitchen. He did not look happy.

"Where have you been?" he asked.

"A few of us went out after. For dinner."

"Was it better than the dinner you were supposed to be home for?"

And it wasn't until then that I remembered—a Family Dinner. I had promised, and I had forgotten.

"Your mother is very upset," my father added.

"Well, I'm sorry," I got out.

"You don't sound very sorry."

There was no winning. None whatsoever.

"I'm going to bed," I told him.

"You will be home for dinner tomorrow. Do you understand?"

"It's not that difficult a concept."

"What did you say?"

"I said fine. *Fine*."

The next day at class, Federica had us doing exercises most of the time, so I didn't get a chance to have Graham Time by myself. I did notice him watching me, though. Singling me out. At one point I winked at him and he laughed.

I was home in time for dinner, but not in time to set the table. Jeremy had done it dutifully in my place.

As soon as the food was served, conversation turned immediately to the Bar Mitzvah. Reply cards were in, and with less than two weeks to go until the big day, it looked like there were more attendees than my parents had been planning on.

"All your cousins are bringing their boyfriends," my mother said with a sigh. "I knew we shouldn't have let them bring a guest. All it takes is one of the girls to bring a boyfriend, and suddenly they all have boyfriends to bring. We haven't even met these boys. Except for that Evan, and he was *not* family material."

I don't know what started me thinking. Maybe it was the fact that two of my cousins were exactly my age. Maybe it was the notion of *family material*. But suddenly I was involved in the conversation. Suddenly I had something to say.

"I didn't know Diane and Liz were allowed to bring guests," I said.

"Yes, and Debbie and Elena. You knew that."

I put down my fork. "So I assume this means that I can bring a guest too."

Now my father put down his fork. "What do you mean?" he asked with a tone of genuine mystification.

"I mean, I can bring someone. Right?"

"But these are the girls' boyfriends," my mother said.

"What about *my* boyfriend?" I found myself asking.

Pure silence at the table, loud shouting in each of our heads. Except Jeremy's. He just watched, transfixed.

"What boyfriend?" my mother asked.

"He doesn't have a boyfriend," my father answered. "He's just being stubborn."

"His name is Graham," I said. "He's in my dance class."

It was the name that did it. The name that made it real. For all of us.

"Jesus Christ," my father said, pushing his plate away.

"There are already too many people," my mother added quickly, somewhere between diplomatic and petrified. "There isn't enough room."

"There's room for Diane's and Liz's and Debbie's and Elena's boyfriends."

"But that's different."

"How is that different?"

"It just is."

"That's bullshit."

Now my father looked truly pissed. My mother was still trying to salvage her argument. "We don't even know this boy," she said, having already forgotten his name. "It's not like you've brought him home for us to meet."

That was brilliant. "Why in God's name would I want to do that?" I was shouting now, near tears. Trying desperately to keep those tears in, so they wouldn't see them.

"Honey . . ." my mother soothed. But it was too late for her to make it better.

"Don't leave this table," my father said.

So I left. Threw my napkin on my plate, went to my room, closed the door.

How many times had we acted this out before?

Usually I slammed the door. Locked it.

I was beyond that now. I wanted it so that they wouldn't hear a thing.

Like I was already gone.

If I'd had a car, I would have driven all night. But instead I let my mind do the driving. It took me to Graham's apartment. Into his arms. He was telling me everything would be okay.

My mother knocked and told me there was still food in the kitchen.

I didn't answer.

My father walked by. I could hear his footsteps slow for a second, then move on.

When Jeremy came by, his knock was quiet, as if he thought I was already asleep. Because I felt bad he'd had to see everything, I told him to come in.

He stayed in the doorway. Was it because he didn't want to disturb me? Or was he afraid I'd shout at him too?

I didn't know.

I was about to apologize for dinner, to let him know it

really didn't have anything to do with his Bar Mitzvah. But he surprised me by speaking first.

"Do you love him?" he asked.

"Who?"

"Graham."

He was serious. I could see it on his face. He was trying to process it all, and he was serious.

"Yes," I said. "I probably do."

He nodded, and I knew there was probably something else that I should say. But once again, I didn't know what those words were. I wasn't used to being a brother.

And that nod. Was he accepting me? Or was it about something else? He looked determined. But I had no idea why.

"Good night," he said, closing the door.

I had planned on sneaking away in the morning, avoiding them all. But when I got to the kitchen, Jeremy was already there, our parents in orbit around him, trying to get their things ready for work. Neither of my parents said anything about the previous night. Neither acknowledged that this was anything but an ordinary day. But Jeremy . . . well, Jeremy did.

He didn't even look up from his Frosted Flakes.

"You're going to let Jon bring Graham to the Bar Mitzvah, right?" he said between spoonfuls.

My parents shot each other a glance. Then my father said plainly, "No, we're not."

Jeremy, still looking at his cereal: "Why not?"

"It's not appropriate. If this were a few months ago,

maybe. If this was a longtime thing, perhaps. But not now."

"How do you know how long it's been?" I asked.

But my father didn't rise to the question. He just said, "End of discussion."

Now Jeremy raised his eyes from his breakfast and looked straight at our mother.

"I want to invite Graham," he said.

"That's sweet," she replied. "But really, it's too late."

Jeremy went on. "If you don't want to invite him as Jon's date, he could come as one of my friends. I know Herschel can't make it, so Graham can come instead."

Instead of answering my brother, my father went after me. "What have you been saying to him?" he asked. Then, turning to Jeremy, "What did he say to you?"

"He didn't say anything to me," Jeremy answered. "I just think if Jon wants to bring his boyfriend, he should."

"The answer," my father insisted, "is no."

He gathered up his briefcase, as if this truly was the end of discussion. My mother and I stood still, waiting—for what, we didn't know. I watched Jeremy. He looked pained. I wanted to tell him to stop, it was okay. But I stayed silent and he did not. He looked right at my father this time.

"If Jon can't invite Graham," he said slowly, "then I am not having a Bar Mitzvah."

"What?" my father asked, as if he hadn't heard right.

"You don't have to do this," I said.

"No," Jeremy told me. "I do."

Why? I had done nothing to deserve this. Nothing.

"We'll talk about this tonight," my father said before storming out. He didn't even kiss my mother good-bye, like he always did.

My mother looked at me and said, "You see what you've done?"

I couldn't take it. I know I should have stayed by Jeremy's side. I should have talked to him. Maybe talked him out of it. But it was too much. I did the only thing I knew how to do—I left. I gave Jeremy a squeeze on the shoulder—that's what I could give him. And I gave my mother a kiss, probably because my father hadn't. Then I was out of there. Free, but not.

I was in a daze through school and the trip into the city, but seeing Graham brought me to all of my senses. At first I wanted to tell him everything. Then I just wanted to tell him something. And eventually I would have been satisfied with telling him anything. We worked pretty much the whole day together, the same Blur songs playing over and over as he led me through the steps, as I showed him what I could do. His sweat on mine, his hand guiding my body. I felt such sureness there. Nobody could tell me what I was doing was wrong.

Thomas invited some of us to stay at his house overnight. His parents were away and he wanted to have a party. We didn't trust Thomas to catch us from our leaps, to make the right entrance at the right time, but we did trust his parents to have a large, unlocked liquor cabinet and plenty of space to crash.

It was Friday. There was no reason for me to go home, and plenty of reasons for me to stay.

I called the house and Jeremy picked up.

"Tell Mom and Dad I'm staying over at my friend Thomas's," I told him. I even gave him the number.

He took it down, repeated it to me. We hung on the line for a second.

"Hey, Jon?"

"Yeah?"

"Are you really going to Thomas's?"

"Yeah."

"Not Graham's?"

I heard a little hope in his voice. "Nah," I said, "but I'm hoping he'll be there. Thanks again, by the way, for this morning. You really don't have to do that."

"No, I want to," he assured me. "It's important."

I was trying to think of something to say in response, but Jeremy quickly told me our mother had gotten home, so he had to go.

I told Thomas I was in the clear, then I went to find Graham. He'd just changed from the shower, his hair dripping perfectly.

"A bunch of us are going to Thomas's," I said, all casual. "You wanna come?"

I thought for a moment he was going to say yes, his smile was such a welcome one. But then he shook his head and said he had other plans. *A date*? I wondered to myself.

"A friend's birthday party," he said, as if reading my fears.

So a bunch of us went up to Thomas's—Miles and I were the only sleepover guests; the rest were all city kids. Thomas's place was nearly palatial, an Upper East Side mansion-apartment. We had the run of the land. Soon we were drinking, flipping cable channels, and gossiping about all the people who weren't there. For one night— this big-city night—I was an adult and I was treated like an adult. Like my opinion mattered. Like I had things to say. Like I could do what I wanted because I could judge my own consequences. We started talking about families and I bragged to everyone about what my brother had done, made it sound like we'd both stood up to our parents. Of course, I didn't tell them who I'd named as my boyfriend, or even that I'd given him a name. I made it an argument over principle—an argument I'd won.

"So what's going on with you and Graham?" Miles asked later on, when we took over the bunk beds in the guest room. Everyone else had left by now, except for Eve, who was making out with Thomas. A kind of host gift. I thought Miles was a little bit drunk and I wasn't sure whether or not I was too. I knew Graham would tell me, if only he was here.

"I don't know what's going on with me and Graham," I said—and Miles laughed. "What?" I asked.

"Nothing," he said. And then his voice changed to another voice, a gentler voice, as he wished me good night.

The next morning—more like afternoon, really—we woke up before Thomas. Miles cleaned the living room while I took a shower. Then another hour passed and Thomas still hadn't emerged from his room. There was no way we were going to interrupt his closed door, so the two of us decided it was safe to leave. I asked Miles what he wanted to do.

"Why don't we check out where Graham lives, see if he's around?" he replied.

"But we don't know where he lives!" I protested.

"Ooh, look," he said, picking up the phone, "I got some magic in my fingers. I just press 411 and"—he gave Graham's name and the East Village and asked for the address—"presto!"

There were messages on my cell phone from my home number, but I didn't check them. My parents' voices didn't belong anywhere near this world. As Miles and I rode the 6 train downtown, we tried to piece together all the events of the previous night. Miles seemed disappointed in Thomas, and I wondered if he had a crush on him. (I hadn't known Thomas was into girls, but I hadn't really cared either.)

I didn't think we were actually going to show up at Graham's doorstep. But when we got there—he lived next to a pizza place on East Ninth—Miles headed straight for the bell.

"What are you doing?" I asked, not without some alarm.

"Don't you want to see if he's in?" he replied. I couldn't tell if he was taunting me or just trying to help.

"I'd rather just bump into him," I said.

So we got a pizza, then wandered around the block a half-dozen times, until a lady on the stoop next to his asked us what the hell we were doing.

Neither of us wanted to go home, so we dragged our wandering farther, checking out the tattoo parlors on St. Mark's and getting an overpriced latte to share at the Starbucks on Astor Place. Finally we found ourselves back at the dance studio—we were allowed to use it on weekends for rehearsal. It was better than going home.

And there he was. We walked into the studio and Graham was the only one there. Dancing each part of his piece, rehearsing for all of us at once. I felt such intimacy toward him then. An intimacy that was stolen, yes. Like staring at someone dreaming.

I watched him, and I could feel Miles watching me watch him. I didn't try to hide it.

It was only when the dance was through, when the sound track had moved on to the next song, that Graham looked over and we made our presence known. Applauding, Miles and I walked into the room. Graham seemed surprised to see us, but not unhappy.

"So you survived your momentary brush with the lifestyles of the rich and infamous?" he asked. We told him a little about the party. He didn't talk about *his* party, but he did say that his friends hadn't made it to a midnight showing of a movie he wanted to see.

"We should go," I said.

"Cool." Graham looked at me. "You free now?"

"Yeah," I said, trying not to sound too eager.

"Miles?"

And Miles did the most amazing thing. He said, "No, I gotta get home. You two'll have to make do without me."

Part of me was afraid Graham would use this as an excuse to back out. He said he was sorry Miles had to go. And he asked me if I could wait ten minutes while he showered and changed.

I said it wouldn't be a problem.

"Thank you," I said to Miles as soon as Graham hit the changing rooms.

He shook his head. "I don't know which of us is the bigger fool."

I asked him if he was really going home. He just shrugged and said, "We'll see. I gave away my shift, but maybe I can get it back."

Graham came out of the changing room with his shirt unbuttoned one step lower than most guys would have dared. I was wearing a black stretch tee made for a dancer's figure. We were quite a pair, entirely in place on the SoHo streets. On the ten-minute walk to the theater, we talked mostly about the dance and how it was coming along. When we got to the box office, he insisted on buying my ticket. I got us sodas.

The movie didn't matter. As far as I was concerned, it existed to give us its glow in the darkness, to give us faint voices to hear at a distance from our thoughts. I wished I had gotten us only one soda. I moved mine so the center armrest would be free and clear. The theater was almost empty, the movie at the end of its run. I tried to focus on the scenery on the screen—the English manor house, the droll goings-on. But it was Graham, Graham, Graham. Right beside me. Only a gesture away.

His arm was on the armrest. I moved mine closer. Then closer still, so our sleeves were touching. He was looking at the movie, but he was feeling me closer. And closer. I turned to him. He turned to me. I moved my hand on his. I traced my fingers around his fingers, then ran them down his sleeve, down his arm.

He pulled away.

I wasn't ready for his movement. The choreography suddenly confused me. This was the wrong improvisation. He pretended to be moving for his soda. When he put it down, he kept his arm in his lap and his eyes on the screen.

Two more hours. The movie lasted two more hours.

When it was over and the credits were rolling, he leaned over and asked me what I thought, if I was ready to go. *Ready* was the last thing I felt, but *go* was pretty much at the top of the list.

He wasn't going to say anything. For a second I wondered if my mind was playing tricks, if what had happened hadn't really happened after all. But once we were in the lobby, once we were in everyday light again, I could see the awkwardness of his stance, his expression.

When you dance, you measure distance as if it's a solid thing; you make precise judgments every time two bodies exist in relation to each other. So I knew right away the definition of the space between us.

We moved to the street, the rest of the audience dispersing in animated clusters around us. It was still daylight, but it was almost dark.

"Jon," he said. Just the way he said my name. Every part of me but my hope gave up right then.

"But why?" I asked.

He put his hand on my shoulder, and even now I loved that.

"I really think you're fantastic," he told me. "But I think you might have the wrong idea."

Later on, I would want elaboration—every possible kind of elaboration. But right then, I only wanted to leave. He asked me if I was okay. He asked me if I wanted to get coffee, or talk some more. He was kind, and that made it better and made it a whole lot worse. I had to go.

I walked around the city a little, but even that was too much. I took the train home, defeated. The only saving grace was that my parents were already out when I got home.

Jeremy was there, though, babysitting himself, which wasn't something I'd been allowed to do. He was watching TV, studying his Torah portion during the commercials.

"Hey," he called out when he heard me come in. "How was it?"

At first I didn't know what he meant—how was what? The movie? The date? The ride home?

Then I realized he meant the sleepover at Thomas's. Which he thought I'd spent with Graham.

"It was okay," I said, throwing my bag down on the floor and sitting next to him on the couch. He muted the TV.

"Did you have fun? Did you tell Graham about the Bar Mitzvah?"

"Look," I said, "I don't think that's going to happen."

"No, it is!" Jeremy said, looking totally energized. "Mom and Dad gave in. I knew they would."

I couldn't believe what I was hearing.

"How?" I asked.

"I just told them I wouldn't do it," he said. "And they knew I wouldn't."

"Are you kidding?"

He looked at me, confused. "No. Not at all. It seemed stupid to have a Bar Mitzvah if I wasn't going to stand up for something that's right, you know."

I knew he was trying to help. I knew he was trying to take my side. But still I couldn't help but see him as my younger, inexperienced brother who didn't know anything about anything.

"Do you understand what you're doing?" I said, my voice rising. I wanted to shake him. "Don't think I don't appreciate it. But are you crazy? Think about it for a second. Not about Mom or Dad. Or me. Think about you. This is a very big deal, Jeremy. All our family. All your friends. Do you really want all your friends to see your brother and his boyfriend? There has to be a line somewhere, doesn't there? Do we get to sit together? What do I introduce him as? Do we get to dance together? What do you think everyone will say, Jeremy? Your Bar Mitzvah will go down in history as *The One with the Gay Brother and His Boyfriend*. You can't want that. You can't."

But even as I was saying it, I was looking at his expression and I was thinking, *Yes, he does. He is ready for all of that.*

I didn't know where he got it from. Not my father or mother. Or me.

"Jon," he said, "it's okay. Really, it's okay."

This twelve-year-old. This stranger. This brother. This person sitting on the couch with me.

It was too much. I had to leave again. Only this time I wished I had the ability to stay. I wished I could stay there and believe him.

But it was too much. It was all too much.

I tried to sleep through Sunday. My mother came into my room and asked me to try on my suit one more time.

"I have to hand it to your brother," she said. "He makes one hell of an argument. Especially when he's right. Sometimes I guess you need to be bullied by the truth. I was caught up in everything else." Then she smiled at me and apologized for how stressful the past few weeks had been. "I just want to live through it," she said, straightening my tie. "I want it to be a perfect day. Although at this point I'd settle for really good."

She asked me if I'd asked Graham. I said yes.

She asked me if he was coming.

I said yes.

It's not that I wasn't thinking—I was thinking way too much. I was thinking of what Jeremy was willing to do, and how I'd be letting him down if I didn't deliver on the situation I'd thrown him into.

"Does he know to wear a suit?" my mother asked.

Again, yes.

She put her hand to my cheek and said, "I look forward to meeting him."

I knew that took a lot.

I thanked her.

My father let his lack of complaint speak for him.

The whole day I wanted to pull Jeremy aside and tell him: *You're believing in love more than I do. You're standing up for someone who is less than deserving.*

I was trying to keep my mind from Graham, from Monday afternoon, when we'd see each other again, but that was an impossible thing to do. Every hour that passed was loaded with thousands of thoughts—and no conclusions.

Somehow I made it through school. Somehow I made it into the city. Somehow I walked through the door to class without trembling.

He was waiting for me, waiting with Eve and Miles to rehearse the third movement of the Blur piece.

"Hi," he said, a little hesitant. Then, after he sent Eve and Miles to rehearse in a corner together, "How are you?"

"Been better," I said. "I'm really sorry—"

"No, I'm sorry. I didn't mean to give you the wrong idea. And at the same time, I don't want you to think I don't care about you. I do."

"I know," I said. Maybe I did, maybe I didn't. Maybe he did, maybe he didn't.

We hovered around our apologies, our acceptances.

"It's okay," I said finally. "Really, it's okay."

Maybe I even believed that. But my body didn't. It had lost the thread of the dance, grasping instead at ulterior intangibles. My arms opened too wide, then held too fast. My turns ended in the wrong place.

Graham did not say a word. Not until Eve and Miles were involved. Then he tried to minimize the damage I was doing, the errors of my way.

I could sense Miles watching me, wondering what had gone wrong. But Graham was always within hearing distance. It wasn't until after the dismal rehearsal that Miles could come over, put his hand on my shoulder, and ask me, "What happened?"

He took me to a used bookstore café around the corner. He bought me tea. He sat me down. He didn't ask what happened again, because any fool could tell. The language of my posture all translated to defeat.

"Jon," he said. Quietly, gently, the word pillowing out to me.

And I told him. What had happened, what hadn't happened. Even more than I'd realized before. Eventually I found I was talking more about Jeremy than I was about Graham. About how I had set up this picture in my brother's head of what my life was like, and how he had fought for that picture. That had made it more real. And I couldn't deal with it. I was still running away instead of fighting too.

"Your brother's pretty brave," he said. "I can't imagine . . . "

I waited for him to finish the sentence. What couldn't he imagine? Doing it himself, or having someone do it for him? I waited, but he left it open, closed.

I looked at him, studied the thoughts that I could see coming through his expression, right underneath. Most dancers find their confidence in dancing. Right is mere millimeters away from wrong. Failure is always louder than success. But there is an accumulation of all the things you don't do wrong, and that becomes your confidence. You can even get to the point where that confidence lasts longer than the dance. Seconds at first. Then minutes. Then maybe it'll be there when you're walking into a party, or meeting people after a show. You know you have something desirable and you know you can move. But for Miles, the confidence wasn't there. Instead, there was something even more marvelous—the trying.

Suddenly, it occurred to me. I was looking at Miles twisting the coffee stirrer around his paper cup. I was thinking of him, of me, of Jeremy.

"You could be my boyfriend," I told him.

"I could?" The coffee stirrer fell to the table, still looped.

"For the Bar Mitzvah. You could be my boyfriend. Would you?"

"Be your boyfriend?"

"For the Bar Mitzvah."

Miles looked at me strangely. "That's one hell of a proposal," he said.

"C'mon . . . it'll be fun."

"Now, you *know* that's a lie."

"Are you free?"

"Are you crazy?"

"Please."

"You want me to pose as your boyfriend—the boyfriend you've never had—in order to make sure your brother—God bless him—didn't take a stand for nothing?"

"Pretty please," I said.

"You're so stupid. You know I'm going to do it."

For the first time that awful day, I felt something approximating happiness. "I will owe you," I told Miles. "Anything your big heart desires."

"Anything?"

He seemed happy despite himself.

And so it came to pass that on the morning of my brother's Bar Mitzvah, I was introducing Miles to my parents as Graham, but telling them to call him Miles, since that was what all his friends did.

He looked amazing, in a blue suit, white shirt, and purple tie. He'd taken a train, a bus, a subway, and a cab to get to the synagogue, and he'd made it exactly on time. My parents, overwhelmed by all the greetings coming their way, were polite without really registering. Jeremy pulled away from the rabbi to shake Miles's hand, to tell him he was glad he'd come. He turned to me and said Miles was exactly what he'd pictured. I didn't know what to say.

Miles was going to sit in the back, but I wanted him beside me. So we sat in the front row. When his *keepa* kept falling off his head, I reached up and pulled out one of the bobby pins keeping my *keepa* in place. Instead of handing it over, I leaned into him and touched his hair, securing the *keepa*. Maybe nobody was looking, but it felt like everyone was. I didn't turn to see what was true. I just looked at him and his nervous smile.

The service began, and all focus turned to Jeremy. It was so strange to sit there and watch him for two hours. I don't think I'd ever really *watched* him before. It wasn't that I hadn't realized he was growing up—I was always waiting for the next stage, the first hint of body hair, the voice's awkward, jagged plunge. But I was always mapping him out against my own progression—as if he were somehow having the same life just because he had all the same teachers. Now I wasn't seeing him in terms of age, or in terms of me. I was just seeing him. Five years behind me, but somehow with his shit together. He'd tied his tie himself and it was perfectly knotted. He chanted over the Torah portion as if it were something he was born to do. And he made eye contact. I swear, as he spoke it was like he looked each of us in the eye. Bringing us together.

I should have felt proud, but instead I felt awful. That I had let him down so many times, that I had been a horrible brother. That he loved me anyway. That maybe he knew more about life than I did, even if I'd had more experience. Because knowing about life is really about knowing how it should be, not just how it is.

It hadn't occurred to me that this would be Miles's first Bar Mitzvah; it hadn't occurred to me that he might be more nervous than I was. During the rabbi's sermon, his leg started to shake. I rested my hand on it for a second, giving him as much of my calm as I could. He accepted it without a word. I used the open prayer book as a phrase book to tell him things, pointing to words, rearranging the scripture to spell out our own verse. GOOD. IS. PLENTIFUL. YOU. ARE. ALL. WISDOM. SHINING ON A HILL.

When the service was over, when we were all getting up to shuffle to the reception, he straightened my tie and moved some of the hair from in front of my eyes. My mirror. I fixed the back of his collar. His mirror.

Jeremy had sneaked into the reception hall before the service, banishing one of our cousins to a kids' table so Miles could sit with our family. I wondered what we looked like to him, as we said our prayers and lit our candles and danced a whirlwind hora. I tried to put myself in his place, and realized we looked exactly like what we were: a family. These strangely tied together individuals trying desperately to keep both ourselves and one another happy. Succeeding, and failing, and succeeding.

When Jeremy called me up to light one of the thirteen candles on the cake, he said the kindest things, and I knew he meant each and every one. He talked about me teaching him how to ride a bike, how to swim, how to kick an arcade game in just the right place to get a free play. He was remembering the best of me. The way he spoke, I almost recognized who he was talking about.

I stayed up for the final candle, for my parents at their proudest. The love I felt for them then—I knew I meant that too. It wasn't something I had to think about. It was there, unexpectedly deep. I hadn't been running away from that, or even from them. I had been so focused on my destination that I'd forgotten all the rest.

At the table, my mother asked Miles how long he'd been dancing. They talked *Nutcrackers* while my father watched, taking it in. After the hora, the dancing grew more scattered, the sincere thirteen-year-old girls and the jesting thirteen-year-old boys doing their sways and muddles as my older aunts and uncles kicked up (or off) their heels and used the same moves they'd learned for their weddings decades ago.

Miles and I watched from the sidelines, and I gave him the anecdotal tour of my family's cast of characters. At one point Jeremy came over and asked, "So, are you guys going to dance or what?" But I wasn't sure Miles wanted to, so I put it off. Miles was doing me enough of a favor. Dragging him onto such a dance floor would be cruel.

I tried to imagine Graham there in his place, but I couldn't. It was laughable. Impossible. Stupid.

Finally, after two or three songs of sitting in the folded-chair gallery, picking at the mixed salad with blueberry balsamic vinaigrette, Miles turned to me and said mischievously, "So . . . are we going to dance or what?"

"Yes," I said. "Let's."

Miles smiled. "It's about time."

Just because two people can dance well on a stage to prearranged choreography doesn't guarantee that they will be good partners in a simple slow dance. When Miles took my hand in his, there was no guarantee that our arms would fit right. When he put his other arm around my back, there was no guarantee that it would feel anything but awkward, unrehearsed. When his feet started to move, there was no guarantee that my steps would match his.

But they did.

As if we had rehearsed. As if our bodies were meant to be this. As if we were meant to be this. Together.

He closed his eyes. He was with me, he was elsewhere, he was with me. I looked over his shoulder. My mother smiled at me and I nearly cried. My aunt and uncle smiled. Jeremy watched, as a girl tugged on his sleeve, telling him to hurry.

I closed my eyes too.

The sound of a dance. This dance. The ballad of family conversations, clinking glasses, plates being cleared. One heartbeat. Two heartbeats. The song you hear, and all the things beside it that you dance to.

When it was over, Miles pressed my back lightly and I squeezed his hand. Then we separated for a fast song.

Instead of jumping off the dance floor, we jumped into the fray. We joined Jeremy and his friends, the aunts and the uncles. We electric slid. We celebrated good times (come on). We cried *Mony, Mony*. As a crowd, part of the crowd, together.

It was fun.

When the next slow song came on, there was no question. I reached for him, and he let me.

"May I?" I asked.

"Certainly," he replied.

But just as we were about to start, there was a tap on my shoulder. I looked to my side and saw it was Jeremy.

"May I have this dance?" he asked.

I let go of Miles and turned fully to my brother, raising my hand to his.

"Uh . . . sure," I said.

Jeremy looked at me as if I were an idiot. "Not with you," he said. "With Miles."

My brother wanted to dance with my not-quite-but-maybe-so boyfriend. I could imagine all his friends watching—his eighth-grade friends watching. Talking. Our family. Our parents.

"Why?" I asked.

He winked at me. I swear to God, he winked at me. And then he said, "I want to make Tom insanely jealous."

"Let's go, then," Miles said, laughing. And with that, they left me. Stunned. They took the dance floor, laughing and awkward and wonderful. I felt such love for both of them. Such love.

I looked over to Jeremy's friends, who were all watching. I wondered which of the boys was Tom. If Jeremy was serious. Then I looked over at my father, at everyone else who was watching, confused and excited. Something was happening. I knew my father would blame me. I knew he would say all of this was my fault. And I would take it. I couldn't take any of the credit for my astonishing brother, but I would happily take all of the blame. If it could be in some way my fault, then I would know I'd done something right.

I would stay to find out. And stay, and stay, and stay.

It is never, I hope, too late to be a good brother.

FEAR

BY TERRY TRUEMAN

Alphonso "Zo" Driggers is fourteen years old. He is
taller than a lot of kids his age in the neighborhood,
taller and thinner. He has lived in the same place since
he was born. Two weeks ago, his mother, who lives
alone with Zo in their small clapboard house, finally
decided to install security bars on the windows and
expensive security doors on both the front and back.
Their house has been burglarized four times in the last
three and a half years, the last time, three weeks ago,
while both Zo and his mom were sleeping. That night,
the burglars came in, stole the twenty-five-inch flat-
screen color TV Zo's mother had purchased just six
weeks before (the fourth TV in as many years), a
portable CD player, and even some jewelry from the
small blue jewelry box Zo's mother keeps on the top of

her headboard, only a few feet away from where she was sleeping.

Zo's father is not around. He never has been. Zo has not seen his dad for quite a while, the last time being Christmas three years ago, when his father had shown up unexpectedly, drunk and acting stupid. Zo's mother had only let Zo's dad stay for a few minutes, then he had left. His dad had not brought Zo any gifts, but he had slipped him a ten-dollar bill on his way out the door. At the time, Zo thought that he would never spend that money, that he'd keep it forever to remind him of his dad. But the lure of candy and of buying popcorn for all his friends at the school popcorn sale had proven too much of a temptation to resist—soon the ten was ancient history, just like Zo's dad.

It is a school night, a Tuesday, in early February. Zo's mother, who works as a checker in a grocery store, has an evening shift—something that doesn't happen very often. Zo is home alone. For the most part, he doesn't mind. He has some schoolwork to do, but with his mom gone, he turns on MTV and watches videos. It's a dark night; a winter breeze is blowing along the street outside—not cold, but not warm either. There is a dark feeling to the evening.

Zo gets a bowl of ice cream and sits down on the couch. An older video is playing. As he lifts a soupspoon of ice cream toward his mouth, a big bite of Rocky Road, suddenly Zo hears something. It's a very distinctive sound, and he recognizes it instantly. Somebody outside is messing with the window in the spare bedroom at the back of the house, the room that his mother uses for sewing.

Zo freezes. He quietly lowers the spoon back into the bowl and sets it on the table in front of him. Moving as silently as he can, he tiptoes over to the hall closet where his aluminum baseball bat leans against the wall just inside the door. He quietly pulls the bat out and grips it. His mother doesn't own any guns.

There are more sounds from the back of the house; Zo can now hear the window squeak as it is pushed up and open. The door to that room is closed, but it's a weak door, loosely hanging on old hinges. There is over an inch of space between the bottom of the door and the floor.

Zo moves silently down the hall, avoiding spots where he knows the floor creaks. He edges his way along the wall, so that whoever is out there won't see his footsteps in the light, which shines into the darkened room from beneath the door.

Suddenly, Zo hears a whispered voice from outside.

"She's got bars up!" the voice says.

"I can see that, man, pull 'em outta the way."

"You pull 'em; they're strong."

Zo hears a slight creaking sound and a soft grunt. Then more creaking and another grunt, then quiet cursing. There is silence for several moments. Zo hopes and prays that they have gone away. Maybe the bars were too much, maybe they . . .

"HEY, ALPO!" a voice calls from the back door, several

feet to the east of the window where they have been try-ing to break in. "Open up this door. We need to get something."

Zo hears a mean laugh, low and cold. "Yeah, Al-phon-zooo," comes a second voice, higher pitched than the first. "Open up."

Zo slides down the wall against which he's been lean-ing. He pulls his knees up to his chest and forms a small ball there on the floor. He's frozen with fear. His legs are rubber, his armpits drip sweat, and his palms are soaked as he tries to grip the taped handle of the baseball bat. His arms turn to lead; he wonders how he'll ever find the strength to even stand up, much less to swing the bat hard enough to do any damage to anybody. He knows there are at least two of them out there; they might have weapons. They seem to know him and how afraid he is.

A terrible uncontrollable quivering grips his body. As he looks across the room at the telephone, he wonders if he could crawl that far and call for help. But lots of times the police don't come into this neighborhood at this time of night unless they have to, and when they do come, it's almost always too late, almost always after a crime has already been committed.

One of the voices outside seems to read his mind. "Don't be thinking about calling the police, Alpo—the police don't care about you. Besides, you go phoning the cops, can't handle your own stuff, you know that's weak. The word gets out that you bring the police around, you know—that's weak-ass, Alpo!"

The other voice laughs again. "You know that's the truth, Alpo," he says, pauses a second, then laughs again, an angry, horrible laugh, then says, mean and low, "Open up this damn door!"

There is a vague familiarity to the voices. Where has Zo heard them before? It could be anywhere, the 7-Eleven or the nearby playground with its rusted hoops and metal nets. It could be anywhere and it could be anyone. How can he make them go away? How can he save himself? He's too afraid to even think.

Fear. Zo hates his fear. He forces himself to his feet and walks, almost in a trance, toward the back door of the house. He stands at the door, tears rolling down his face as he reaches his hand toward the bolt lock, ready to twist it open. His fingers touch the metal handle. It's cold. In the grip of his terror, he can't think of anything else to do.

In another second, he could turn the lock and these intruders would come in. Zo feels such shame at his cowardice; he knows he is a coward. He pauses and tries to catch a breath. Thinking about his shame, he realizes and flashes in an instant, "I'd rather be dead than this afraid."

"I said open this door, Alpo! We know you, and you're not gonna stop us. Open up now, and we won't hurt you. You make us get mean and we'll get you, maybe tonight, maybe tomorrow, but trust me, Alpo, we'll get you."

Zo whispers to himself again, "I'd rather be dead than this afraid." He takes another deep breath and pulls his hand back from the lock. "I'd rather be dead than this afraid." Something happens inside his chest—somehow he is able to breathe again, able to think. And now he feels angry. "I'd rather be dead," he whispers.

"We'll get you, Alpo!" the voice says again, full of hate and menace.

"You might," Zo answers back, surprised by the strength of his voice.

"No 'might,' we will!" The voice is cold and murderous.

"You think I don't know you?" Zo says. "You think I can't find out who you are?"

"So what?" one of the voices answers. "You can't do anything!" They both laugh.

"Can't, huh?" Zo snaps back.

The first voice speaks again, another mean laugh in his words. "Oh right, you're all tough and bad, huh?" They laugh again.

Zo pauses for another second, takes another deep breath and speaks low and angrily. "I will call the cops. I'll tell them a couple losers are trying to rob us—I'll tell them that you threatened me, said you're gonna kill me. Everyone in the neighborhood will know that you're the kind of guys who try to scare a kid who's home all alone. Is that what you want? Is that how you're gonna build up your rep? Anything happens to me, the cops will find you. You think you're bad enough to handle that?" Zo pauses a moment to let his questions sink in, now he laughs his own mean laugh. "I don't think so! You say another word, I'll call 'em. Period."

There is a long moment of silence. The voices from

outside are quiet. Finally one of them speaks, the mean-ness gone. "The cops don't care about you, boy—"

Zo interrupts loudly, his voice strong and defiant. "They care about guys like *you*!" he snaps back. "I let you in here, let you steal our stuff while I sit here like a little baby, hell, I might as well be dead anyways. But if I call the cops, get them after you—you'll be the ones who are scared! If you think I'm lying, count ten seconds and lis-ten for sirens—I'm gonna call 911 right now!"

Zo hears another moment of silence, then, just outside the door, a hushed, hurried whispering.

Finally the first voice speaks again. "All right, Alpo, hold on, take it easy. Forget about it. Just keep the cops out of this, okay? Just chill. We were just playing with you anyway—relax, you know, don't worry about any-thing Alpo, just—"

Zo interrupts, "My name is Zo, not Alpo!"

Zo waits for a response, but in the next moment he hears only the sound of the chain-link fence rattling as the strangers leap over it and then run away into the darkness.

Walking back to the couch, he sits back down and glances at his bowl of ice cream—it hasn't even melted too badly yet. As he picks it up, he smiles to himself. "That's Zo, not Alpo! My name is Zo!"

IT'S COMPLICATED

BY RON KOERTGE

Sean's outside the abandoned cabin in Tieman's woods. He's so still, the animals take him for granted. A couple of high-performance squirrels do Cirque de Soleil stunts in the big oaks. He knows if he were to squirm even a little, everything—birds, bunnies, you name it—would crouch or scatter. He doesn't want that.

He still comes here, he does and Megan does, though their friends think it's kid stuff, so they've moved on. Whatever that means. His dad uses that on him, that "moved on" stuff. Which he claims he had to do once his wife left to—this is so embarrassing—find herself.

"I don't know who I am," she'd wailed.

Well, Sean knew who she was: his mother.

She just looked at him. "Besides that."

It's summer. June. He thinks of the house. His house. His and his dad's. Of how he left it thirty minutes ago. Of how he keeps it spotless. Perfect. For when she comes back.

He's got yellow rubber gloves for dishes, blue ones for hard cleaning like in the bathrooms. He owns two or three kinds of bleach and a vacuum with an engine like a sports car, which his dad willingly bought since Sean never asks for anything. Never, in fact, talks to his father unless absolutely necessary.

He sits with the sun on his face and waits for Megan with her cap of red hair. Her freckles. Thousands of freckles. All of which she showed him one day when they were twelve. After which, quid pro quo, he unveiled his wiry body: no big deal. Then, anyway.

What about now? What if they did that now? Man, who knows. Well, they talked about it (they talk about everything). And agreed their friendship was too valuable. The companionship. The partnership, almost. The welcome sight of each other. Hours on the phone. Hours in the woods, at the movies, on the court.

The other way, the erotic way, the kissing and the groping way, well—they knew where that led: How many girls had they seen at high school crying in the hall, their friends patting and smoothing them like snowmen? How many guys had smashed their fists into their lockers, then gone out and wrecked their cars?

That seemed stupid. He'd seen his dad cry, heard his mother's endless interrogations.

No, that's not for him. This is for him: a warm day, dishes done, laundry folded, waiting. Again. As usual. Like always.

For Megan. Whom he hears at exactly the same time as do the fauna. They freeze: Sean and the squirrels. Then there she is: perfect for the forest—red hair, black shirt, white pants. Audubon could have drawn her. Held his breath first in awe and admiration.

Except for those big earphones. There's something on the Discman hooked to her belt, and Sean knows she wants the song to end just as she steps into the clearing.

He watches her Converse high-tops. There's a tiny Band-Aid on one shin where she cut herself shaving. Unlike most girls, Megan likes to shave her legs. Likes Sean to sit with her while she does it. Or wants him to do it.

She always wears Bermudas or long cutoffs, so it's intimate but not sexy. It could be, but they don't let it. She sits on the side of the tub. He on the toilet seat (closed). She puts one leg out. He pretends the razor is a snowplow and clears a road to Knee Mountain. If he keeps pretending, he's okay. If he admits it's a real knee—smooth and warm—and below that a muscled calf and above that a just about perfect thigh . . . well, that was teetering on the edge of what they'd agreed not to do.

When she sees him, she smiles and down come those earphones. She looks like a disc jockey or air traffic controller. "Hey."

He just nods like Brad Pitt might. Or John Cusak. Somebody cool.

She's wearing lip gloss, and it's not perfect. Which is somehow better.

She says, "I was thinking last night after we hung up that when we go trekking in Tibet like we were saying we might and it's really cold and you freeze to death, I'll only be able to eat your arm but not your face. I like your face too much."

"Megan, if there was a fire so you could cook my arm, I wouldn't freeze to death."

"I need to go pee. Is there any toilet paper in the cabin?"

Sean likes it that she asks him. It's intimate and honest as well as slightly gross. He gets up, fetches what's there—half a roll, gray and puckered.

"Don't go anywhere!" She sounds stern. "Or no candy later."

Megan is always doing that—switching roles, play-acting. Shape-shifting, sort of. To her, it's like trying on clothes. And she's good at it. Is that why he loves her, because there's so many different Megans?

His dad is worried about Sean, about the intensity of his friendship with Megan. "It's not smart," Dad says, "to put all your eggs in one basket."

Sean knows it makes his dad nervous when he doesn't answer, so he doesn't answer. He just stares at him. Not that there's much to stare at: hair like yellow grass, a purple birthmark (small but unavoidably there) on his forehead, and soft all over.

Sean really has nothing but scorn for his father. Why hadn't he been a better husband? Smarter, wittier, more attentive, more affectionate? More of whatever it was his mother wanted.

Eggs in one basket. Megan wasn't an egg. His heart wasn't a basket. Did his dad really want him to have half a dozen friends stashed away so if something happened, there would always be another one waiting in the wings? That wasn't friendship, that was backup!

While Megan's gone, Sean thinks of his spotless house again. Imagines his mom coming back. Being impressed. Dad dropping the new girlfriend.

He hears Megan. Watches as she ducks into the cabin, then reappears and slides down beside him, propping herself against the splintered boards.

"Anything new from your father, that fountain of wisdom?"

He quotes, "'It's complicated.'"

"That's what he said last time."

"And the time before."

"Well, I don't get it. I tell you everything, you tell me everything, we see each other every day. But no way is it complicated."

"He says I'll understand when I'm older."

"They always say that."

She turns his way. Turns lazily. Doesn't lift her head off

the weathered boards, but lets it roll. It's a summertime move, done at the pool a lot.

He says, "I kind of want to kiss you."

"I know."

"But we don't do that."

"Yeah." She gets to her feet like immediately. Lightning fast but graceful and silent. "Let's shoot some hoops."

They walk out of the woods single file. Like always. Being as quiet as possible. They had moccasins once. Bows and arrows. Now they're stealthy in Nikes and Converse. Their trusty steeds have two wheels; they're old enough to drive (Megan has a car, an old Subaru), but they prefer their mountain bikes. The cardio they get from pedaling everywhere. His Huffy is pretty basic, but Megan's is stripped down to frame, tires, pedals. Like her when she runs track.

The gravel road is first: past the Wilson farm, the long curve by old Bethel Church. A stretch with no houses, just soy beans. Then one or two places with a yard dog, then a house every hundred yards or so, then the mail-boxes-with-little-red-flags stop and they're in a neighbor-hood. Two blocks from the nearest playground.

Their hometown is rurban: rural/urban. Ten minutes by car in three directions and it's cows, crops, tractors. But they also have a computer store on Main Street, a four-plex cinema, coffee shop that sells cappuccino and blank journals for the chronically sensitive, lots of churches, lots of bars. Some people make the sixty-mile drive to Springfield to eat out, but not often. Usually it's

Sizzler or Pizza Hut. Clothes shopping is different; there's at least a Gap in Springfield. Locally there's just The Toggery, and doesn't the name just say everything? Togs, for God's sake. Megan and Sean shop by catalog: L.L. Bean, Lands' End, Eddie Bauer, and that Sierra place, the discount one.

In fact, Sean's wearing new cargo shorts from Sierra, cool ones with about eleven pockets but very lightweight. He needs new sneaks, but won't give up the old ones because his mom bought them, shopped with him, got down on her knees when he first tried them on and pressed his big toe to make sure they fit.

He doesn't like thinking about his mom, but he's afraid if he stops, she's gone forever. So he remembers that shoe store. Her high spirits in the mall that day. How she put her arm through his, how she wanted to make sure the shoes were just what he wanted. How she fussed over him, asked him to walk around. Then she got down on one knee and pressed and probed and lifted his right foot and to keep his balance he put one hand on her head. The feel of her hair. The slow-motion stream of it.

Megan steps off her bike, lets it fall. Handlebars twisted up like that, it looks like a downed animal. A deer maybe. Sean parks his, kickstand and everything.

Megan does a few jumping jacks. Windmills her arms. Stands at the free throw line and sinks three out of five. Tries a few loping layups.

"One on one." She cannons the ball at him, two-handed. "You're out."

He's not very good at this. Megan is faster than he. A better shot. Plus the game matters more to her.

He dribbles calmly. She's poised like a wrestler: crouched, arms out. He doesn't even move, just *Boom!* And drains one from downtown.

"Sweet."

He taps her clenched fist, relieved. Takes his place. Gets ready to lose.

They play to 21 twice. It's 21–11, then 19–9. He's got no D. He's got no jump shot. She fakes him out one last time and scores.

"Good game!" Her eyes are green with gold flecks. She drapes an arm around his neck. She's sweaty but still smells good

"Don't forget," she whispers, "to say your prayers."

"For sure."

She mounts her bike and is gone.

Sean cruises the main street's buffet of churches. Holy Family is the most prosperous. There's a big rectory next door, then a block of stately two-stories. Elm trees. Screened-in porches.

He started dropping by Holy Family pretty soon after his mom left. The church soothed him: always cool, plenty of flickering candles, stained glass everywhere.

As usual he goes right to the pew nearest the statue of the Blessed Virgin. That swimming-pool blue robe. Those kind eyes. He sits, hands in his lap.

"Sean?"

He doesn't look up, just nods.

"Sean, your mother is sorry she had to leave. Very sorry." The voice is sweet and musical without being gooey. "She's in Florida now. She hasn't got a boyfriend or anything like that. She thinks of you a lot. All the time. She has a reason, a good one, for not writing."

He talks down into his clasped hands. "She's okay?"

"She's got a suntan and everything. The place she's staying temporarily has lots of wicker furniture and a breeze. She's a waitress in a nice restaurant. The salary is okay, but the tips are great. She keeps them in a jar with your name on it. She's saving up to send for you."

Sean and Megan are playing basketball with their high school's only anarchists: Bernard and Chris/Kris. The latter likes to spell his name with a *K* because he thinks that's more anti-everything. Bernard can't wrest any anarchism out of his name, but won't be called Bernie.

Sean gets a kick out of these poseurs, sweating in their dog collars and Doc Martens. As a team, he and Megan are pretty good. He boxes out, she drives hard. He shoots from outside.

Then a Saab convertible pulls up. The girl who gets out sports those long NWBA shorts that aren't short at all. She's got a red and white basketball that she spins so the colors blur. She's not black, but not white either. Puerto Rican, maybe. Or some Tiger Woods medley. Exotic for sure.

And quiet. Just sits down, back against the chain-link fence. Everybody's self-conscious, watching her watch them. She wears what look like reading glasses perched on the end of her nose. But she's not reading.

Bernard can't stand it, so he fakes a sprain. "Take my spot," he says, hobbling off the court toward an ancient, splintered bench.

She turns out to be good. Really good. Excellent. And Kris is to her as Sean is to Megan. Only less so. Kris can't hit from outside. The new girl drives around Sean at will. At top speed, she leans like a guy racing motorcycles: She's so close to the ground, her shorts touch the asphalt.

After the game (21–17 her and Kris) she holds out one hand. To Megan. Says one word, "Lily."

Sean waits for Megan's joke, because Lily is all wrong; no way is she a Lily. But what he gets is reverence.

"Man, where'd you learn how to play like that. Lily."

He hears Megan tack the name on at the end. Getting used to it. How it feels in her mouth.

"Around." Lily looks at Megan. At the convertible. "Want to go for a ride?"

"We'd love to."

Lily doesn't even look at Sean. "Whatever."

He climbs in back (that's a foregone conclusion). Settles into the leather. Likes it in spite of himself.

"What's to do around here?" Sean hears it, but she's talking only to Megan.

He thinks of the new-kid-in-town movies he's seen: Kevin Bacon in *Footloose*. Christian Slater in *Pump Up the Volume*. He thinks of chemistry. Unstable elements. He sees himself in a white coat holding the neck of a shattered beaker, his hair on end, soot all over his face. Best to make light of the situation. Make it into a cartoon. Something he can turn off.

In spite of the wind and the cranked-up radio (it's hip-hop, which Sean hates), he learns that Lily is from L.A. Her dad is an eye surgeon who makes the drive to Springfield. After a divorce, he wanted Lily in a more wholesome environment. And miles away from Mom.

But Sean feels like a dog at the conversational table: All he gets is whatever Megan slips him when nobody's looking. Sean closes his eyes. Wakes up when Lily hits the brakes hard. They're back at the playground.

"Those your bikes?" she asks, peering over her very cool shades. "They'd be gone in sixty seconds where I come from."

Said like she's proud of that. Like she misses danger and peril.

"Throw yours in the back, Meg. I'll take you home."

It's not Meg. It's never Meg. She hates Meg. She'll bust Lily for that.

"Cool."

Sean is out of the car. He didn't vault like he wanted to, but he didn't slither either. "I think I'll go to church now."

Megan hesitates. "Later might be better."

Lily doesn't look at either of them. She just races the engine. He offers to help Megan load the bike, but she waves him away.

At home, the phone messages are for his dad. From the girlfriend. The home wrecker. They're bland, domestic.

Pick up some milk, okay? Stuff like that. Sean's father lives with her, and he doesn't. He's home, and he's not.

Sean tries not to hate him too much. He doesn't want to end up taking the bus to Springfield to see a therapist like some kids do.

His dad calls. He's going to eat dinner with Sheila tonight. At her place. Does Sean want to come?

Sean does not. He doesn't mention the milk.

The phone rings. It's Megan. Has to be.

"She makes me feel like I've been living under a rock!"

It's Megan, all right. Not even a hello.

"Why is that?"

"Are you kidding? She's been everywhere, done everything. Doesn't she just make you want to get a passport and get out of here?"

"No."

"She could be gay too. Maybe. And you know what I know about that? Willow from *Buffy the Vampire Slayer*. That's what I know about that. Am I boring you? Is this boring? Let's talk about something else."

"Fine."

"Do you know she played with the pros in summer league? And she wants to get drafted right out of college. What do the girls around here want? Either to take their prize heifer to the state fair and win a blue ribbon or get married."

Sean tries to believe everything isn't ruined or awful but just different. "What about us?" he asks. "What's this got to do with us?"

"It's not like that. I'm just, you know, smitten."

"What about me?" He can't help saying it, but he hates how it came out.

"Maybe you should pray."

That gets his attention. He blurts, "Really?" Hears the eagerness. Thinks, *Pathetic.*

"For sure," she says. "Like today around four."

Sean puts his hands on the back of the pew just ahead of him, leans his forehead on them. Listens.

"Your mother has a better job, so there's more money. She can come and get you pretty soon. She's eating healthy and getting enough sleep. She sends her love. Waves of it. One after the other. More than you can count."

It's what he wants to hear, but not the way he wants to hear it. It's too hurried. Too by-the-numbers. Not as soothing. It reminds him of his mother saying "I'll always love you" while she's putting things in a suitcase.

That's pretty much the last time for the Virgin Mary. Megan doesn't call as often either. And when she does, all she can talk about is Lily.

The hell with her.

He starts playing pickup ball with whoever. Older guys most of the time. For his trouble, he takes an elbow or two, gets tripped up, goes down hard. He pedals home slowly to pick gravel out of his own thigh.

He acquires a small rep as a deadly outside shooter and, on his own, practices some inside moves to quash their expectations. He sees Megan around. She's leaner, harder, doing some rigorous regime with Lily, no doubt. Running a thousand miles. Lifting a ton. Stuff like that.

Lily's dad is gone a lot. Megan's folks have always been apparitions: ghost parents. The girls are always together. Lily's volatile, jealous, possessive. Megan's always upset. She avoids him but leaves cryptic messages. Complaints mostly. But she stays. Doesn't break it off. Doesn't tell Lily to go to hell.

He continues to play ball, to get better. To like it more for its own sake, not just because Megan liked it. He continues to go to church and just sit too. He's there one day in July. Liking the cool atmosphere because he's hot from the playground. Hot from winning. And from clocking some guy with pores so big, his nose looked like an asteroid. This guy fouled him repeatedly. And clumsily. That made it worse. So he let him have it.

He's sitting, making his mind an ice rink. A thought skates out, he watches it, then banishes it. His hand aches a little. Fighting is not his thing; it always hurts more than in the movies. Still, that guy asked for it.

"Sean."

He's startled. Looks to his right. At the statue of Mary. It's a voice he doesn't recognize. Blue. Does that make any sense? A blue voice.

"I don't know if your mother's coming back or not. I was wrong to tell you that she was. That was a mistake and I'm sorry. I'm sorry for a whole lot of things. Lily's moving. So that's that. I just feel stupid. Don't be too mad if you can help it. Your dad turns out to be right. Things are really complicated."

Sean can't help himself. He bolts from the pew, scaring one of the old ladies who are always in the back praying. But there's nobody. Not behind the statue. Not making her way out.

He leans on the virgin. Feels the cool plaster. Puts one hand on the hem of her robe. Takes a few deep breaths.

That thing she just said about his mother not coming back? He'd pretty much decided that on his own. *Don't be too mad if you can help it.* He was, though. A little, anyway. But as mad at himself as he was at her. When all this started with Lily, shouldn't he have been with Megan like he was with that guy who kept fouling him and just got in her face? It's easy to say she should have known he loved her. But he never actually told her.

Man, who knows. Really.

He should go home, take a shower, get hold of his dad, go to dinner with him and his girlfriend. Whom he met last week. And was polite to.

He'll call Megan, just not right now.

Sean crosses himself and leaves. Outside, he stands on the steps. Bounces a little on his toes. His strong legs. His own two feet.

ABOUT THE GUYS

PAUL ACAMPORA

WHEN DO YOU THINK YOU WENT FROM BOY TO GUY?

WHEN THE NURSE PUT OUR FIRST CHILD, MY SON, INTO MY ARMS . . . I NEVER IMAGINED THAT AN EVENT WITHOUT COCKROACHES OR PLANE CRASHES COULD SCARE ME THAT MUCH . . . UNTIL WE HAD A GIRL.

WHAT'S THE MANLIEST THING YOU DO NOW?

I PRETEND THAT MY DAUGHTER WILL NEVER GROW UP. I'M A PRETTY STRICT DAD. I LIKE TO FISH AND KAYAK. I TRY TO BE GOOD AT WHAT I DO. SOME DAYS IT WORKS OUT.

WHO'S THE MANLIEST GUY YOU'VE EVER MET, AND WHY?

THE MANLIEST MAN WOULD BE MY FATHER'S FATHER. HE GREW UP ON A FARM IN ITALY AND THEN WORKED IN A FACTORY MOST OF HIS LIFE. HE RAISED A GARDEN IN CONNECTICUT THAT WAS AS BIG AS HALF A CITY BLOCK. GRAPES, MELONS, LETTUCE, CARROTS—THERE WAS NOTHING HE COULDN'T GROW. WHEN HE WALKED BY HIS FRUIT TREES, FIGS AND PEARS AND APPLES WOULD BURST INTO BLOOM FOR FEAR THAT HE'D TAKE A SAW TO THEIR BRANCHES. UNDER HIS COMMAND, EGGPLANTS AND PEPPERS AND TOMATOES GREW AS BIG AS HORSES' HEADS. ONE DAY HE MADE ME HELP HIM SLAUGHTER CHICKENS. AFTER WE STACKED A DOZEN DEAD HENS ON A WORKBENCH, I OBSERVED THAT THEY WERE ALL LYING AS STILL AS, WELL, DEAD THINGS. "BUT I THOUGHT CHICKENS WERE SUPPOSED TO RUN AROUND AFTER YOU CHOP OFF THEIR HEADS," I SAID. MY GRANDFATHER WIPED A BLOODY HAND ON THE CHECKED APRON HE'D SNUCK OUT OF MY GRANDMOTHER'S KITCHEN. "WHEN I KILL THE CHICKEN," HE TOLD ME, "THE CHICKEN STAYS DEAD." IT TAKES A REAL MAN TO LOOK THAT TOUGH IN AN APRON.

PAUL ACAMPORA'S FIRST NOVEL, <u>DEFINING DULCIE</u>, WILL BE PUBLISHED BY DIAL BOOKS IN 2006.

EDWARD AVERETT

WHEN DO YOU THINK YOU WENT FROM BOY TO GUY?

MY BRAIN IS STILL WAITING FOR THAT MAGICAL TRANSFORMATION FROM BOY TO GUY. I LOOK IN THE MIRROR AND THINK THERE MUST BE SOME MISTAKE. SOMEBODY FORGOT TO TELL MY BRAIN THAT I'M GETTING "MORE MATURE."

WHO'S THE COOLEST GUY YOU'VE EVER MET, AND WHY?

THE COOLEST GUY I EVER MET WAS THE LATE AMERICAN PAINTER ROBERT HARVEY. WHEN I WAS LIVING IN SPAIN AND TRYING TO OPEN A BANK ACCOUNT, HE WENT WITH ME AND HELPED ME THROUGH THE PROCESS. THE BANK MANAGER WAS FILLING OUT A FORM FOR ME AND ASKED WHAT MY OCCUPATION WAS. I WAS TRULY STUMPED. ROBERT JUST LOOKED AT ME AND SAID, "WHY, YOU'RE A WRITER, OF COURSE." THAT WAS MY FRIEND ROBERT HARVEY. HE ALWAYS KNEW MORE ABOUT ME THAN I DID. I'VE BEEN A WRITER EVER SINCE.

EDWARD AVERETT'S FIRST YA NOVEL, <u>THE RHYMING SEASON</u>, WILL BE PUBLISHED BY CLARION BOOKS IN 2005.

RON KOERTGE

WHAT'S THE MANLIEST THING YOU DO NOW?

FOR ME IT'S PROBABLY BETTING MORE THAN I CAN AFFORD TO LOSE AT THE RACETRACK. I ASSOCIATE ADULTHOOD WITH A CAPACITY FOR FOOLISHNESS. I'M NOT THE SORT WHO LIKES TO LOSE (THERE ARE THOSE), BUT I LIKE TO PUT MYSELF IN JEOPARDY.

WHO'S THE COOLEST GUY YOU'VE EVER MET, AND WHY?

THE COOLEST GUY I KNOW IS THE FORMER POET LAUREATE BILLY COLLINS. HE'S ENORMOUSLY SUCCESSFUL BUT MODEST, GENEROUS TO YOUNGER WRITERS. HE'S ALSO VERY WITTY AND—THOUGH HE HASN'T SMOKED FOR YEARS—ALWAYS SEEMS TO BE HOLDING A CIGARETTE. WHENEVER I SEE HIM IT SEEMS TO BE ABOUT 7:00 P.M. AND THERE'S THE WHOLE NIGHT AHEAD OF US.

RON KOERTGE HAS WRITTEN MANY BOOKS, INCLUDING THE BRIMSTONE JOURNALS, STONER AND SPAZ, SHAKESPEARE BATS CLEANUP, MARGAUX WITH AN X, AND THE ARIZONA KID.

DAVID LEVITHAN

WHEN DO YOU THINK YOU WENT FROM BOY TO GUY?

HMM, THERE'S NO PARTICULAR MOMENT THAT I WENT FROM BOY TO GUY (AND I DON'T THINK I'D EVER REFER TO MYSELF AS "GUY" ANYWAY).

WHAT'S THE MANLIEST THING YOU DO NOW?

I HONESTLY CAN'T FIGURE OUT A WAY TO ANSWER THIS QUESTION. I WOULD NEVER ANSWER A QUESTION ABOUT "MANLY" THINGS BECAUSE I THINK THE WHOLE NOTION IS KIND OF STUPID AND I DON'T WANT TO REINFORCE IT IN ANY WAY.

WHO'S THE COOLEST GUY YOU'VE EVER MET/CAN REMEMBER, AND WHY?

MOST OF THE COOLEST GUYS I KNOW ARE WOMEN. AND MOST OF THE COOLEST GALS I KNOW ARE MEN.

DAVID LEVITHAN IS THE AUTHOR OF <u>BOY MEETS BOY</u>, <u>THE REALM OF POSSIBILITY</u>, AND <u>ARE WE THERE YET?</u>. HIS STORY IS DEDICATED TO DAVID, LAUREN AND JOHN.

WHEN DO YOU THINK YOU WENT FROM BOY TO GUY?

WHEN MY HAIR STARTED TO FALL OUT. FORTUNATELY, I HAD MY GAL BY THEN.

WHAT'S THE MANLIEST THING YOU DO NOW?

I OPEN JARS WITH MY BARE HANDS. IF THERE AREN'T ANY JARS THAT NEED OPENING, I GO FISHING.

WHO'S THE COOLEST GUY YOU'VE EVER MET/CAN REMEMBER, AND WHY?

BRUCE COVILLE, BECAUSE HE'S SMART AND FUNNY, AND HE WRITES AMAZING BOOKS.

DAVID LUBAR IS THE AUTHOR OF MANY BOOKS, INCLUDING <u>FLIP</u>, <u>DUNK</u>, <u>HIDDEN TALENTS</u>, <u>WIZARDS OF THE GAME</u>, <u>IN THE LAND OF THE LAWN WEENIES AND OTHER MISADVENTURES</u> AND THE UPCOMING <u>INVASION OF THE ROAD WEENIES AND OTHER TWISTED TALES</u>, AND THE MOST RECENT, <u>SLEEPING FRESHMEN NEVER LIE</u>.

WHEN DO YOU THINK YOU WENT FROM BOY TO GUY?

THE DAY I HAD TO CLEAN OUT THE CAB OF A MILITARY TRUCK IN WHICH THREE YOUNG SOLDIERS HAD BEEN KILLED WAS THE DAY I UNDERSTOOD HOW EASY DEATH CAME. FROM THAT DAY ON I WAS, IN MY MIND, A GUY.

WHAT'S THE MANLIEST THING YOU DO NOW?

THE MANLIEST THING I DO IS TO MENTOR YOUNG WRITERS—NO EGO INVOLVEMENT, NOTHING TO PROVE.

WHO'S THE COOLEST GUY YOU'VE EVER MET/CAN REMEMBER, AND WHY?

WILLIS REED, FORMER KNICK STAR. A GEN-UINELY WARM AND GIVING INDIVIDUAL WHO GAVE ME SOME INSIGHTS ON A BOOK I HAD JUST FINISHED. HE LIKED THE BOOK, BUT POINTED OUT HOW CEREBRAL PARTS OF IT WERE. MY NEXT BOOK WAS BETTER BECAUSE OF THE ADVICE OF THIS 6' 7" DUDE.

WALTER DEAN MYERS IS THE AWARD-WINNING AUTHOR OF MONSTER, HANDBOOK FOR BOYS: A NOVEL, BAD BOY: A MEMOIR, FALLEN ANGELS, SHOOTER AND MANY OTHER BOOKS FOR YOUNG READERS.

WHEN DO YOU THINK YOU WENT FROM BOY TO GUY?

EVEN THOUGH I HAVE NEVER BEATEN MY DAD AT ARM WRESTLING, I CAME CLOSE WHEN I WAS IN HIGH SCHOOL. THAT WAS A KEY MOMENT IN MY MATURING. I THOUGHT, WHAT'LL HAPPEN IF I BEAT THE GUY WHO I'VE ALWAYS THOUGHT WAS THE STRONGEST MAN IN THE WORLD? IT THREW ME FOR A LOOP.

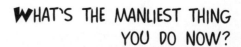

WHAT'S THE MANLIEST THING YOU DO NOW?

I CHANGE MY BOY LUKAS'S DIAPERS AND KISS AND HUG ALL OVER HIM. I NEVER DID CARE FOR MY OWN DAD BEING ALL HUGGY WITH ME WHEN I WAS A YOUNG GUY, AND NOW I REGRET BEING STANDOFFISH WITH HIM ABOUT IT, ESPECIALLY WHEN HE WANTED TO HUG ME IN PUBLIC, AND IN FRONT OF MY FRIENDS WAS EVEN WORSE. BUT NOW I KNOW WHAT HE WAS FEELING, BECAUSE HUGGING LUKAS MAKES ME HAPPY, SO HAPPY I THINK I'LL EXPLODE.

RENÉ SALDAÑA, JR., IS THE AUTHOR OF THE JUMPING TREE AND FINDING OUR WAY.

CRAIG THOMPSON

WHEN DO YOU THINK YOU WENT FROM BOY TO GUY?

I BELIEVE I BECAME A "GUY" WHEN I SERIOUSLY STARTED INTERACTING WITH GIRLS. NOT WHEN I FIRST BECAME INTERESTED IN GIRLS (THAT WAS ACTUALLY A QUITE AWKWARD AND BOY-ISH TIME), AND NOT MY FIRST ROMANTIC RELATIONSHIP WITH A GIRL (THAT'S SOMETHING DIFFERENT ALTOGETHER), BUT WHEN I WAS ABLE TO SPEND TIME AND CONVERSE AND LEARN TO IDENTIFY WITH THE OPPOSITE SEX.

WHAT'S THE MANLIEST THING YOU DO NOW?

I DID A LOT OF AGRICULTURAL WORK WHEN I WAS YOUNGER, AND THAT WAS PRETTY MANLY—DRIVING TRACTORS, BALING HAY, SETTING UP FENCE POSTS—BUT NOW MY LIFESTYLE'S NOT SO TOUGH AND MASCULINE. FOR SOME REASON, I FEEL MANLY WHEN I HELP PUSH SOMEONE'S CAR THAT'S BROKEN/STUCK, OR LIFT LITTLE KIDS ONTO MY SHOULDERS.

WHO'S THE COOLEST GUY YOU'VE EVER MET/CAN REMEMBER, AND WHY?

MY FRIEND DAN IS A PRETTY DAMN COOL GUY. HE'S PAINTED ONE PAINTING A DAY FOR SEVEN YEARS, AND MAKES A HEALTHY LIVING AT IT, AND IS TOTALLY HUMBLE AND UNPRETENTIOUS ABOUT THE FACT. IN THE ART WORLD, IT'S INCREDIBLY RARE TO FIND SOMEONE WHO IS "ALL WALK, RATHER THAN TALK" WITH A DOWN-TO-EARTH ATTITUDE ABOUT WHAT THEY DO.

CRAIG THOMPSON IS THE AUTHOR AND ILLUS-TRATOR OF THE GRAPHIC NOVELS BLANKETS; GOODBYE, CHUNKY RICE; AND HIS MOST RECENT, CARNET DE VOYAGE.

WHEN DO YOU THINK YOU WENT FROM BOY TO GUY?

MY MOM WOULD HAVE TOLD YOU I WAS STILL A BOY WHEN I WAS 23 YEARS OLD AND MOVED AWAY TO AUSTRALIA FOR A COUPLE YEARS, BUT THAT I CAME BACK A MAN . . . SHE MIGHTA MEANT MY HAIRLINE, SEEING AS HOW I MUST HAVE BEEN ALLERGIC TO THE WATER OR SOMETHING, BECAUSE I CAME BACK PRETTY BALDING.

WHAT'S THE MANLIEST THING YOU'VE EVER DONE?

I DID A VERY BRAVE THING ONCE THAT I CAN'T TALK ABOUT, WON'T TALK ABOUT, AND IT ISN'T FUN OR FUNNY ANYWAY, SO NEVER MIND, BUT I DID IT. OTHER THAN THAT, I ONCE CALLED OUT A COLLEGE PROFESSOR WHO WAS BEING RUDE AND OBNOXIOUS TO A WOMAN FRIEND. I ASKED HIM TO "STEP OUTSIDE OR SHUT UP!" I DUNNO, SHE CALLED ME HER KNIGHT IN SHINING ARMOR, BUT SHE LAUGHED A LOT WHEN SHE SAID IT. THIS WAS KINDA MANLY CAUSE I WAS THEN (AS I AM NOW) UTTERLY WEAK AND PROBABLY WOULDA GOTTEN DESTROYED.

WHO'S THE COOLEST GUY YOU'VE EVER MET/CAN REMEMBER, AND WHY?

I'VE MET A LOT OF COOL GUYS WHO WERE ALL COOL IN DIFFERENT WAYS: CHRIS CRUTCHER AND TERRY DAVIS, NOT ACTUALLY COOL AT ALL, WHICH IS PRETTY COOL; CRAIG T. NELSON, COOL DRIVER OF FAST CARS; KEN KESEY, INCREDIBLY BRAVE AND SMART COOL GUY; STUDS TERKEL, FUNNY LITTLE OLD COOL GUY — THE COOLEST OF ALL, HOWEVER, IS MY SON, JESSE CRUZ TRUEMAN, WHO, ALTHOUGH NOT ALWAYS COOL, ALMOST ALWAYS IS AND WHO WAS VOTED THE "COOLEST KID" IN HIS SIXTH-GRADE CLASSROOM—YEAH, JESSE, FOR SURE!

TERRY TRUEMAN IS THE AWARD-WINNING AUTHOR OF <u>STUCK IN NEUTRAL</u> AND <u>CRUISE CONTROL</u>.

MO WILLEMS

WHEN DO YOU THINK YOU WENT FROM BOY TO GUY?

11:43 P.M. GMT, JUNE 12TH, 1986, IN THE BATTERSEA SECTION OF LONDON, ENGLAND.

WHAT'S THE MANLIEST THING YOU DO NOW?

I GIVE MY DAUGHTER PIGGYBACK RIDES ON THE WAY TO MINOR-LEAGUE BALL GAMES; THAT'S MANLY.

WHO'S THE COOLEST GUY YOU'VE EVER MET/CAN REMEMBER, AND WHY?

MY DAD WAS PRETTY COOL TO ME AS A KID. HE WAS A GRUFF POTTER WITH VERY STRONG HANDS, AND I WAS FASCINATED BY HIS BALD HEAD AND HAIRY ARMS. ONE DAY, MY DAD TOLD ME THAT HIS ARMS WERE HAIRY BECAUSE ALL OF HIS HAIR HAD RUBBED OFF HIS HEAD AND ATTACHED TO HIS ARMS AFTER A FITFUL NIGHT SLEEPING WITH HIS HEAD ON HIS ARMS. FOR THE NEXT FEW WEEKS, I DILIGENTLY SLEPT WITH MY ARMS UNDER THE SHEETS.

MO WILLEMS CREATED CARTOON NETWORK'S <u>SHEEP IN THE BIG CITY</u> AND HEAD WRITES <u>CODENAME: KIDS NEXT DOOR</u>. HIS BOOKS INCLUDE <u>DON'T LET THE PIGEON DRIVE THE BUS</u> AND <u>KNUFFLE BUNNY: A CAUTIONARY TALE</u>. HE'S MADE COMICS FOR <u>MONKEYSUIT</u>, DC'S <u>BIZARRO'S WORLD</u>, AND DC'S 9/11 ANTHOLOGY.